Bondi Beach Medics

Beachside rescues and sun-kissed romance!

With most of their childhoods spent roaming
Australia's shorelines with their nomadic parents,
Sydney was the only place that the Carlson siblings
made their home.

And now they're back! Living under the same roof
and practicing the medicine they love. Saving lives
in its hospitals and on its beaches. After all,
they never could resist the call of the surf!

Yet as the familiar embrace of Bondi Beach's
coastline welcomes them in life and career,
it's the call of love that could truly make
this place their home.

Discover Poppy's story in
Rescuing the Paramedic's Heart

Read Jet's story in
A Gift to Change His Life

Both available now!

And look out for Daisy's and Lily's stories
Coming soon!

Dear Reader,

Thank you for picking up this book, which is the second in my four-book Bondi Beach Medics series.

This is Jet's story, the Bondi lifeguard living a bachelor lifestyle—until the day Mei Chen reappears. I hope you enjoy their story.

I loved the idea of exploring the lives of the Carlson siblings across a series and I'm excited to see where they go. I promise drama, adversity, love and laughter set against a backdrop of sun, surf and summer at Australia's busiest and most famous beach.

If you missed the first book, *Rescuing the Paramedic's Heart*, it's available as an ebook from your favorite retailer. That is Poppy's story. Still to come, Daisy's and Lily's stories!

I'd love to hear from you if you enjoy this story or any of my others. You can visit my website, emily-forbesauthor.com, or drop me a line at emilyforbes@internode.on.net.

Emily

A GIFT TO CHANGE HIS LIFE

EMILY FORBES

HARLEQUIN

MEDICAL
ROMANCE

HARLEQUIN®
MEDICAL ROMANCE™

Recycling programs
for this product may
not exist in your area.

ISBN-13: 978-1-335-40889-1

A Gift to Change His Life

This edition published by arrangement with Harlequin Books S.A.

For questions and comments about the quality of this book,
please contact us at CustomerService@Harlequin.com.

Harlequin Enterprises ULC
22 Adelaide St. West, 40th Floor
Toronto, Ontario M5H 4E3, Canada
www.Harlequin.com

Printed in U.S.A.

Emily Forbes is an award-winning author of medical romance for Harlequin. She has written over twenty-five books and has twice been a finalist in the Australian Romantic Book of the Year Award, which she won in 2013 for her novel *Sydney Harbor Hospital: Bella's Wishlist.* You can get in touch with Emily at emilyforbes@internode.on.net, or visit her website at emily-forbesauthor.com.

Books by Emily Forbes

Harlequin Medical Romance

Bondi Beach Medics
Rescuing the Paramedic's Heart

London Hospital Midwives
Reunited by Their Secret Daughter

Nurses in the City
Reunited with Her Brooding Surgeon

One Night That Changed Her Life
Falling for His Best Friend
Rescued by the Single Dad
Taming Her Hollywood Playboy
The Army Doc's Secret Princess

Visit the Author Profile page
at Harlequin.com for more titles.

For my children.

I am so proud of you both, and watching you chase
your dreams and achieve your goals
gives me great pleasure. I hope you continue
to live the lives you're dreaming of.

With love, forever,

Mum

**Praise for
Emily Forbes**

"Ms. Forbes has delivered a delightful read in
this book where emotions run high because of
everything this couple go through on their journey
to happy ever after…and where the chemistry
between this couple was strong; the romance was
delightful and had me loving these two together."
—*Harlequin Junkie* on *Rescued by the Single Dad*

CHAPTER ONE

THE SUN WAS starting to drop in the sky, casting shadows over the sand as Jet steered the jet ski past the surf break, parallel to the beach. He kept an eye on the ocean, paying close attention to the three rips that were starting to run as the tide turned.

The jet ski had been launched as a precaution as the late afternoon swell picked up. The long blue rescue boards were hard to manoeuvre over large waves, making it difficult for the lifeguards to get out past the break in an emergency. The motorised ski was faster to respond in big seas but not easy to use when the water was crowded as it was today.

It was the last week of spring, less than five weeks until Christmas, and Bondi Beach was busy. Not anywhere near peak capacity, which could regularly reach forty thousand people at the height of summer, but busy enough to keep the lifeguards on their toes. School had ended for those students in their final year, exams were over and the graduates were making the most of their newfound freedom. Those who hadn't ventured off to the popular hot spots of Bali, the Gold Coast and Byron Bay mingled with the university students, backpackers, tourists and families.

Jet scanned the waves, lifting one arm to shield his eyes from the afternoon sun, as he looked for anything untoward and any sign to indicate swimmers who might get into difficulty—those who weren't strong swimmers or who had overestimated their abilities as well as those who'd been drinking. Alcohol was banned on Bondi Beach but there were several bars in close proximity and Jet knew there would be plenty of beachgoers who had smuggled alcohol onto the sand. While he'd been living in Bondi and working as a lifeguard for the local council for the best part of five years, he had grown up in Byron Bay on the north coast of New South Wales and he'd been part of many end-of-school parties so he knew from experience it was easier to avert disaster than to have to respond to it.

He reached the south end of the bay near Bondi Icebergs, turned the ski one hundred and eighty degrees and headed north. The one-kilometre stretch of beach curved around on his left, bookended by two rugged headlands, while the distinctive circular lifeguard tower held centre stage.

'Jet? We've got a swimmer in trouble near the middle break.' Gibbo's voice came through the radio that was slung across Jet's chest. 'Hands have gone up.'

He pressed the button through the waterproof casing to reply. 'On my way.' He opened up the throttle on the ski and cut through the water.

He scanned the water, looking for raised hands, looking for something to guide him to the site of trouble. Middle break was several hundred metres away and, while he wanted to cover the distance as quickly as possible, he needed to take a wide berth, adding metres to the journey, but his trajectory allowed him to avoid the swimmers and surfers.

There was a man in the water with his hand in the air. He could see people looking in his direction and although he couldn't hear them over the noise of the jet ski it was obvious they were calling for help. He slowed the ski and cut the engine as he drifted in amongst the swimmers. Two swimmers were treading water while they supported a third man between them. The man's face was grey, his eyes were rolled back in his head and he wasn't breathing.

Jet turned around on the seat to face the back of the jet ski and reached into the water. He grabbed the man under his armpits and pulled him onto the rescue mat that was attached to the rear of the ski. He didn't know what had caused the man to lose consciousness and the possibility of a spinal injury hovered in the back of his mind. He hoped he hadn't been speared into the bottom of the ocean by a large wave as there was no option but to drag the man onto the sled and get him back into shore. He couldn't be treated here.

'Can you climb on too?' He nodded at one of the swimmers who had been assisting in the water. 'I need you to hold him onto the board for me, make sure he doesn't fall off.'

The man nodded and Jet helped him out of the water before getting on the radio and calling the tower. 'We've got a resus,' he said. He knew Gibbo would call for an ambulance and send lifeguards down to the water's edge to assist Jet. They would have work to do before the paramedics arrived. 'Send a couple of rescue boards too,' he added. The men who had helped in the water would be fatigued from their efforts. Jet had no idea how competent they were; if they weren't strong swimmers they might need help to get back to the beach and it was always better to pre-empt that rather than wait for another call. Things could turn very nasty very quickly in big seas.

Jet's heart was pounding as he steered the ski towards the sand. There were so many things that could go wrong, and his mind was racing as he sifted through the scenarios. He knew he had to focus. He'd made a decision and now he had to work out what came next. He would still need to get his patient off the rescue mat and onto the beach for treatment.

He needed help but he could see one of the lifeguard buggies racing along the shoreline, coming to meet him. The ATV came to a stop in line with Jet's path and Bluey and Dutchy, two of his fellow lifeguards, were waiting for him as he drove the jet ski onto the sand. A third lifeguard ran past; he was carrying a blue rescue board and was heading into the ocean to check the other swimmers.

Jet jumped off the ski and with Bluey and Dutchy's help lifted the unconscious man off the mat and carried him out of the shallow water and laid him on the hard sand beside the buggy.

He still wasn't breathing.

Jet held his fingers over the man's wrist at the base of his thumb, feeling for a pulse. He moved his fingers around, searching, but there was nothing.

Bluey held the man's head while Jet and Dutchy rolled him onto his side. Salt water poured out of his mouth but he didn't regain consciousness.

The man who had helped bring the patient into shore had followed Jet and the other lifeguards up the beach. 'Do you know him?' Jet asked.

He hadn't stopped to ask that in the water; there hadn't been time and it hadn't mattered then but now he'd like more information. Starting with whether the patient had any pre-existing health conditions. But the other man shook his head.

'Do you have any idea what happened?'

Another shake of the head.

If they weren't going to get any additional information they'd have to treat the patient as best they could.

They rolled the patient back into a supine position so that Jet could begin CPR. Bluey got an airway in and attached a bag ready to pump air into the man's lungs between Jet's compressions.

Dutchy had fetched the kit containing the defibrillator from the buggy and was preparing it for use while Jet counted out his compressions. Dutchy worked around Jet, wiping the patient's chest, drying it off so he could stick the defibrillator pads on.

Jet lifted his head as he continued the compressions. He looked towards Campbell

Parade, hoping to see the flashing lights of an approaching ambulance, but a crowd had gathered to watch the resuscitation effort and they'd formed a wall of people, obscuring his view.

Jet counted to thirty and took a break while Bluey squeezed the bag and Dutchy stuck the defibrillator pads onto the patient's chest. He put his hands back on the patient and resumed his pressure while Dutchy plugged the defib leads into the machine.

'I think I've got a pulse,' Bluey said as Jet sat back, listening to the defib's instructions.

'Analysing rhythm.'

'No shock advised.'

'Yep, definite pulse,' Bluey confirmed.

They rolled their patient onto his side again and this time he vomited and opened his eyes as the crowd clapped and cheered.

Above the noise of the crowd Jet heard the 'toot-toot' of the horn of a second buggy and the wall of people split as the ATV pushed its nose through. Jet could see Ryder Evans, his future brother-in-law, at the wheel, with two paramedics on board.

He recognised the first; Alex often partnered with Jet's sister Poppy, who was Ryder's fiancée, but today she wasn't the other paramedic. The other paramedic, while female, was petite with dark hair. She was the complete opposite to Poppy, who was tall and fair like Jet.

Bluey had strapped an oxygen mask over the patient's nose and mouth and was talking to him, telling him what had happened.

Jet stood up, stretching out his tall, lean frame. He rolled his shoulders to ease the fatigue as Ryder hit the engine's kill switch and Alex and the second paramedic jumped out of the buggy. He frowned as the female paramedic leaned into the back of the ATV and lifted a medical bag out. There was something familiar about her, about the way she moved, but he didn't think he knew her. He wondered if it was just the adrenalin in his system after the rescue and resuscitation heightening his senses, increasing his awareness. His heart was still racing and blood was pumping around his body.

He had a sense of déjà vu as he watched her and a name popped into his head. Mei.

Was it her?

She was wearing sunglasses and a navy cap with 'Ambulance' stitched across the front. Her dark hair was pulled back in a ponytail, her skin was smooth and lightly tanned and her lips were full and pink but that was all he could see of her. It wasn't enough to be certain it was her. He hadn't seen her for years—would he really recognise her after so much time?

She paid him no attention as she gathered her equipment and Jet decided he must be mistaken. He must be confusing her for someone he knew a long time ago.

She knelt in the sand beside the patient as Alex walked over to Jet. Jet knew he needed to give him an account of the incident and of the treatment they had given but he continued to watch the other paramedic while he spoke to Alex. For reasons he couldn't explain he found it impossible not to.

The lifeguard beeped the horn on the buggy and the crowd parted to let them through. This was Mei's fifth day on the job as a Bondi paramedic and her third callout to the famous beach. Although she'd grown up around Bondi she wasn't a fan of the beach, but it was becoming apparent that attending to incidents here would become a regular part of her new job. She'd experienced a traumatic incident in the water when she was young and had tended to avoid the beach after that but, despite this, she had applied for a transfer to Bondi Ambulance Station as it would halve her commuting time. Traffic in Sydney could be a nightmare and working closer to home would give her back precious time to spend with her daughter instead. As a single mother she figured that commuting time could be better spent on more important things.

She hopped out of the buggy, stretching her legs over the blue rescue board hooked along the passenger side, leaned into the back of the ATV to grab her kit bag from beside her colleague and glanced towards the patient. She'd been glad to hear the patient was an adult male; she found dealing with children hard, especially ones around the same age as her daughter. The patient was lying in the recovery position and her heart skipped a beat when she looked that way, but it wasn't the patient who got her all flustered but one of the lifeguards at the scene.

Tall, blond, tanned and lean, he was standing beside the patient. The late afternoon sun shone on him, appearing to deliberately single him out. It was a silly notion, the sun must have been falling on dozens of people but to Mei it felt as if the sun was purposely, and solely, landing on just one person.

Jet.

She'd last seen him eight years ago in Byron Bay on the New South Wales central coast and last she'd heard he had moved to Hawaii. What was he doing on Bondi Beach?

All those sleepless nights she'd spent wondering where he was. All those years when she'd pictured him travelling the world, surely he hadn't been right here, in her own backyard?

What did this mean? Was it fate or fortune? Was his presence going to turn her life around or simply upend it? Whatever happened, she had no doubt it would be life-changing.

The sun made his bronzed skin glow and his golden hair shine. It might have been eight years since she'd seen him, but she'd thought about him every single day with a trace of anger mixed with regret. She waited now for those familiar feelings, but it was nervous excitement that she felt instead. He was even more gorgeous than she remembered and seeing him in the flesh made her heart race and her hands clammy. Her knees wobbled and her breath caught in her throat, just like the first time she'd seen him. They'd been on a beach and he'd been lit by the glow of a bonfire instead of the sun, but she still hadn't been able to take her eyes off him.

But she couldn't afford to let her attention be diverted. Not now. Not again. She had a job to do.

Perhaps he wouldn't recognise her, she thought as she walked towards the patient. She had never forgotten him, but she didn't for one moment expect the same could be said for him. She was wearing sunglasses and a cap, and her uniform was hardly flattering. She suspected she couldn't look more different than the eighteen-year-old girl she'd been when they'd first met. There was no reason for him to remember her. If he didn't recognise her, if he didn't speak to her, she knew she'd be able to maintain focus.

She kept her head down as she went to the patient and knelt in the sand. She and her partner had been given a brief outline of the incident—a successful resuscitation on a middle-aged man.

She could hear Jet summarising the incident for her colleague, Alex. His voice was deep and it coursed through her like music. She felt as if her nerves were guitar strings and each word and syllable plucked at the strings and reverberated through her body. It was an unexpected but pleasant sensation.

But she had other things to focus on, so she tried to block him out. She would work out later how to deal with this surprising turn of events.

She unzipped her bag as she got the patient's name—Paul—from a second lifeguard who had introduced himself as Bluey.

'Paul, my name is Mei; I'm a paramedic.' She talked quietly to him, asking him to squeeze her fingers as she checked for spinal injuries. His grip was strong as he followed her instructions.

She clipped an oximeter to his finger and moved her hands to the soles of his feet. 'Push down against my hands,' she said, relieved to feel responding pressure.

'Do you remember what happened?' she asked the patient as Alex squatted beside her. She resisted the urge to turn her head to see if Jet was still there. She couldn't be concerned about his whereabouts right now.

'Not really. The last thing I remember is a tightness in my chest and difficulty breathing and then I woke up here.'

'He was found floating in the water by some surfers,' Alex told her. 'The priority was getting him to shore.'

She knew what Alex was implying—the priority had been getting Paul out of the water, not looking for spinal injuries.

'Muscle strength is normal,' she said, letting her partner know she had checked. She had done a couple of shifts with Alex, but they were still getting familiar with working together and she knew he couldn't assume that she had performed the right checks. 'But we can pop a cervical collar on, just to be safe.'

Alex nodded and grabbed the collar. 'Just popping this on as a precaution, mate,' he said as he slid it under Paul's neck and fastened the Velcro straps.

'Have you got any history of heart problems?' Mei asked Paul. 'Are you on any medication?'

'No.'

Their priority now was to get Paul stable enough to transfer him to hospital. He needed a cardiac assessment.

'We'll need to take you to hospital. Is there anyone with you?'

'My son is here.'

Mei looked around and saw a young man crouching in the sand to her left, watching the proceedings anxiously. She knew it must be a distressing experience for him. 'If you've got all your things you can come with us,' she told him.

She packed up their equipment as Alex organised the lifeguards to help them roll Paul onto a spinal board, ready to be moved to the buggy.

She knelt in the sand by Paul's right shoulder. Alex was to her left, ready to support

Paul's head as they rolled him. Bluey knelt opposite Mei with Ryder beside him. She felt the air stir as a fourth person knelt beside her. She didn't need to turn her head to know it was Jet. He smelt warm and salty; he smelt of the sun and the sea; he smelt just like she remembered.

Mei kept her gaze fixed on the spinal board, which she held across her knees, ready to slide it under Paul when Bluey and Ryder turned him. Jet reached for the handles in the edge of the board. His fingers brushed against Mei's, making her heart skitter. She kept her eyes averted—she wasn't brave enough to look at him.

Ryder and Bluey had their hands on Paul's shoulders, pelvis and knees, ready to log roll him. 'On three,' Alex issued instructions.

'One, two, three.'

Mei and Jet slid the board under Paul before the others rolled him back.

The moment Paul was safely on the board Jet was on his feet, leaving a void of empty air beside Mei. The air stilled and the energy that had been buzzing around her dissipated as Jet moved away.

She knew she was being ridiculous, but her memories were flooding back. This was the same reaction she'd had to him all those years ago—immediate and completely out of her control. It had been all-consuming, leaving her feeling distracted. Eight years ago, she'd let herself get carried away. She had been looking for excitement, for adventure after graduating from high school and she was overwhelmed by her reaction to Jet and had given herself over to him willingly. But eight years ago she'd been young, naïve and impressionable. None of those things could be said about her now.

She couldn't afford to be irresponsible any more. Her life now was rational, measured. She had responsibilities and commitments; there was no room in her life for fantasies, infatuations or affairs.

She had consigned Jet to history and she'd like him to stay there, even though she knew that was impossible.

There was no way she could ignore him, or the fact that he had changed her life. He had given her the most precious gift. One he had no idea about. They had a daughter. It wasn't a secret she'd intended to keep from him but Jet had disappeared and now, eight years later, she knew she was about to change his life.

They carried Paul to the buggy and loaded him on, ready to transport him across the sand. Bluey drove her, Alex and their patient back to the promenade. Several lifeguards then helped carry the stretcher to the ambulance, but Jet wasn't among them. He stayed down at the water's edge but, even so, Mei's breathing didn't return to normal until she shut the rear doors, closing Alex in with their patient, jumped into the driver's seat and headed to Bondi General Hospital.

She was disappointed but relieved that Jet hadn't recognised her; she wasn't ready to revisit their history. She knew it was inevitable but she needed time to prepare.

She needed to work out how to deal with this unexpected turn of events, but she had time. She had two night shifts coming up and then four days off. She had time to put things in perspective before she would see him again.

She knew what the end result needed to be—she just had to decide the best way to get there.

* * *

Jet stood and watched as Bluey drove down the beach towards the lifeguard tower. The crowd had dispersed and he had a clear view of the buggy as it headed into the distance with the paramedics and their patient. He turned around, knowing he had work to do, but that didn't stop him from wondering about the petite, dark-haired paramedic.

He was disconcerted as he tried to marshal his thoughts. She looked familiar, she felt familiar, but she didn't seem to recognise him. Had it been her?

He helped Ryder pack up the equipment, picking up the detritus and returning the oxygen cylinder and mask to the second buggy. Job finished, he grabbed a drink of water.

'I haven't seen that paramedic before,' he said, trying hard to sound offhand. 'Have you?'

'Nope,' Ryder replied. 'She said she just transferred to Bondi Station a week or so ago. Why?'

'She looked familiar. Did you get her name?'

'May.'

Mei.

It had to be her. Didn't it? But she didn't seem to recognise him. Was it a coincidence? Was that sense of déjà vu simply a figment of his imagination?

He didn't think so——he wasn't given to flights of fancy. But he figured time would tell. The paramedics were called to Bondi Beach frequently, so he'd find out soon enough.

'Do you know her?' Ryder asked.

'I'm not sure.'

He could see from Ryder's expression that his answer wasn't a satisfactory one, but he didn't want to share his thoughts. Something made him hesitate. It had been years since he'd seen Mei—maybe he was mistaken— and he wasn't about to have a discussion about a girl he once knew eight years ago. Ryder would want details. Jet had a reputation for brief dalliances and Ryder would be curious to know what it was about a girl from all those years ago that made her unforgettable. Jet wasn't sure he'd be able to explain.

'I can ask Poppy about her if you like? Or you can. They must have met at work.'

He knew Ryder was fishing but there was nothing he was prepared to say.

Ryder and Jet had grown up together but Ryder had moved from Byron Bay to Perth when they were seventeen. He had left before Jet met Mei and he had never mentioned her to his friend. He wasn't about to mention her now either.

The past was the past. Their relationship had been a fleeting one, like all Jet's relationships. Work and training took up his time. He had been twenty, happily drifting along with vague plans to become a professional surfer. Mei had been eighteen and on holiday in Byron Bay celebrating the end of her school days with friends. They had been chalk and cheese. She was driven, focused and determined but naïve. She had a plan; she set goals that she knew she would achieve. He was a dreamer, a risk-taker, he had no real plans; his priorities were to have fun and spend his days surfing and he'd figured life would take him where he needed to go. But, despite their differences, there had been instant attraction and amazing chemistry and nothing else had mattered.

He wasn't even aware of their differences initially and, to be honest, didn't care. He was interested in her physically, not in her mind. At least not at first, but over the course of seventy-two hours she had challenged him and changed him. And he had changed her.

They had parted ways at the end of the weekend, content to return to their different lives having had a taste of other things, having had their horizons expanded. Mei had experienced spontaneity, she'd relaxed and had perhaps learnt not to be her own harshest critic, that the world wasn't going to end if she took five minutes to enjoy herself. He had learnt that he would need to set some goals and apply himself if he wanted to achieve international surfing success. He'd realised that most people who achieved their dreams had an element of talent, determination and effort to thank, and didn't rely solely on good fortune.

The one thing they did have in common had been loneliness. It wasn't that that drew them together, that had been purely and simply chemistry, but their loneliness had given them a bond, an understanding of each other and that connection had made them feel safe enough to share their thoughts with each other in a way he knew he had never done before.

It was crazy to think that a girl he'd met on the beach in Byron Bay, at a party he hadn't even planned on attending, had managed to have such a profound effect on him.

He had never had a serious relationship, not then and still not now. He'd never felt comfortable expressing his feelings so he'd never been able to give women what they craved—his emotional side. He could share himself physically but opening up emotionally was difficult and he knew it was a barrier to forming a lasting relationship. He told himself he was fine. Told himself he didn't have time, but he craved the attention and recognition he'd never received from his parents.

He'd wanted someone to take him seriously, someone to believe in him. His parents had never been ones to show pride or love or to shower him or his sisters with praise or affection and it was something he longed for. He hated the fact that he felt that way, but he knew that the only way he would get that attention was through his sporting endeavours.

But Mei had been different. Mei had made him feel seen.

They might have been young, and they might have only spent a weekend together, but she had learned more about him in those seventy-two hours than any other woman and taught him more about himself than anyone else ever had.

She'd made him want to be a better person, to strive to achieve. She had made him realise that he couldn't keep hoping for his parents' praise, that he had the chance to set his own goals, to chase his own dreams and to do it for his own satisfaction. Mei had set him on his own path, had freed him to be himself. He hadn't achieved everything he wanted, not yet, but she had been partly responsible for making him who he was today. He wondered what would she think of that.

But that was a long time ago. He wasn't that twenty-year-old with unrealistic expectations any more. He had a career as a lifeguard, which would serve him well for the next few years while he chased his dream of qualifying for the Ironman World Championships. His dreams of becoming a professional surfer had been relatively short-lived and he'd discovered he was far better suited physically to the rigorous, gruelling competition that was the professional Ironman.

He was about to turn twenty-nine; he had years before he needed a serious relationship. In fact, he wasn't convinced he needed one at all and right now he had other things to concentrate on, including two Ironman events in the next month. Mei belonged in the past. He had no time to devote to thinking about her. He was looking forward, not back.

'Do you want me to find out more?' Ryder repeated when Jet didn't respond. 'I'll see Poppy tonight. We're going to look at that rental.'

Ryder and Poppy's relationship was moving at a rapid pace. Apparently they'd had some sort of connection back when they were teenagers, unbeknown to Jet or the other Carlson siblings, but they'd only officially been together for a few weeks. Jet couldn't understand the urgency, but he didn't begrudge Ryder and his sister their happiness. Ryder made Poppy happy, he was a good guy and Jet was glad to welcome him as a brother-in-law. But he didn't envy them. As selfish as it might seem, he was quite content with his bachelor lifestyle.

He shook his head in reply to Ryder. 'Nah. It doesn't matter. I've probably got her confused with someone else.'

'I can believe that.' Ryder laughed as he let the subject drop, just as Jet had intended. His relationships might be fleeting but they were also numerous and he knew Ryder would believe that he'd lose track.

But he knew it was her.

That sense of déjà vu. The spark he'd felt when his hand brushed hers.

He'd been waiting for a sign that she remembered him, but she'd ignored him completely, seemingly unaware of him. He wasn't used to that. He was used to women noticing him and his ego was bruised to think she'd forgotten him.

That, or the alternative—that she knew

exactly who he was but had chosen to ignore him—wounded his pride and he vowed to get her attention.

CHAPTER TWO

FOR THE REST of her shift, each time there was a lull, Mei's mind returned to Jet and the weekend they had spent together and she could think of nothing else on the drive home.

Eight years on and that one weekend felt like a lifetime ago. For her it was. Her life had completely changed in that time. She wondered how different he was.

She'd had no idea he was in Sydney. In Bondi. The last time she'd seen him was in Byron Bay. At the age of twenty he'd been gorgeous, charismatic, full of energy, full of life and she'd been swept off her feet. She'd been ready for some excitement, ready to cast off the stress after years of studying and she'd let herself throw caution to the wind, not concerned with consequences, the future or anything that came next.

She'd never done that before and it had felt liberating.

She'd thought at the time she would be fine, but she should have known better than to tempt fate. She could still hear her mother's voice warning her she would pay the price for any reckless behaviour, for her mistakes, and her mother had been half right. Mei didn't consider her behaviour wayward, it had been her choice, but she hadn't escaped unscathed, although she had learned to live with her mistake. To love her mistake. And she wouldn't change a thing.

Well, almost nothing.

The smell of garlic and spices greeted Mei as she walked from her car to her back door. The dinner service at her parents' restaurant was well underway. Her stomach rumbled as she climbed the stairs to their apartment above the restaurant. She'd shower and change and then go back downstairs and see what her mother was cooking. She hoped the restaurant wasn't too busy. Her mother ran the kitchen and her father ran the front of house with a couple of regular waitresses and if it was busy Mei often lent a hand. But she was tired today. The mental and physical strain of her job had been compounded by the stress of a new environment but, on top of that, seeing Jet again had taken up a lot of her concentration and she wasn't sure she had enough in reserve to be a gracious hostess. Thank God it was Tuesday, usually the quietest night of the week, with most customers opting for takeaway.

Her parents had opened Lao Lao's Kitchen when they emigrated to Australia twenty-four years ago, when Mei was two years old and her brother, Bo, five. Running the restaurant had enabled her parents to raise their children in a new country where they didn't have the extended family support they had been used to in Hong Kong. Mei's parents had worked in one of the five-star hotels—her mother had been a chef, her father was a manager—but he'd had concerns about the future of Hong Kong and together they had made the decision to emigrate and open a restaurant of their own.

Mei and her brother had grown up in the

apartment above the restaurant, but she hadn't ever envisaged that she would still be living with her parents at the age of twenty-six. But then, there were a lot of things about her life that were different to what she'd imagined. She knew her parents didn't mind having her there, but she still dreamt of a life of her own. One day.

Mei slipped her feet into her slides and headed for the restaurant kitchen. If she needed to give her father a hand in the dining room she'd have to change again.

The sound of clattering pans and frying food assailed her as she pushed open the swinging door. Her mother was directing the kitchen staff and didn't notice Mei's entrance.

A young girl sat at the stainless-steel workbench, carefully decanting sauces from a large jug into small condiment bowls. Mei smiled at the look of concentration on An Na's face.

'Hey, gorgeous girl,' she greeted her daughter. She bent down and kissed An Na's forehead.

'Careful, Mummy, you'll make me spill it.'

'Sorry, darling,' Mei replied as An Na looked up and smiled.

Mei caught her breath as Jet's smile flashed across her daughter's face. Albeit missing one front tooth. She'd always known An Na had his smile but seeing it today when Jet's face was fresh in her memory was a jolt she didn't need.

'Hi, Mama,' Mei greeted her own mother as An Na returned to her task.

Mei's mother put chopsticks and a bowl of steamed dumplings in front of her. The dumplings were varied in size and shape.

'I helped Lao Lao make those,' An Na told her. 'They're prawn and chicken.'

Mei remembered being seven and learning to make dumplings. She'd loved the precision of the task, the effort to try to make each one identical. It had taken a long time to master.

'They look delicious,' she said as An Na handed her a bowl of dipping sauce. She knew that even if they were a little mis-shapen they would taste amazing.

Mei gobbled the dumplings as she listened to An Na chatter about her day at school, about the Christmas decorations they were making and the songs she was learning for the Christmas concert.

'Is everything okay? You're very quiet,' her mother asked as she took the empty bowl.

Mei nodded. 'Just a hectic day at work.' It had been busy but that wasn't what was keeping her preoccupied. She wasn't thinking about work and she was only half listening to An Na. She was too busy thinking about Jet.

'Does Dad need help in the restaurant?'

'Not tonight. You can take An Na upstairs—she did her spelling homework with your father after school.'

Mei spent the night tossing and turning over Jet. Every time she closed her eyes visions of him came to mind. His startling blue eyes. The smooth warmth of his bare chest. His long fingers stroking her skin. The taste of his lips on hers. Her hormones were going crazy and it was hard to be annoyed with him when her body was flooded with heat.

She blamed her reaction on the recent lack of sex in her life and told herself it was just a chemical response, but she knew she needed

to stay away from him until she'd worked
out how to maintain her self-control. She'd
dated occasionally over the past eight years,
but not terribly successfully. She didn't want
to be a single mother but she hadn't really
given herself the opportunity to meet someone. It wasn't easy when she still lived with
her parents. Normally dating and sex were
the furthest things from her mind, but seeing Jet again awoke a lot of long-forgotten
feelings and impulses.

It would be okay. She had time to work
out what this meant. What seeing him again
meant. For her but more importantly for An
Na.

In the meantime, she'd have to figure out
how to work with him. She'd been wanting
the transfer to Bondi Station for months; she
couldn't let anything derail her.

'Bondi Eleven, do you copy?'

'This is Bondi Eleven, go ahead,' Mei responded to the ambulance command centre.
She and Alex were heading for the station at
the end of a night shift but, as so often hap-

pened, a call came in before they could get back and hand over to the day shift crew.

'We have a call from the Bondi lifeguards requesting assistance. They have an injured surfer with a nasty gash to the upper thigh; it's bleeding heavily and they haven't been able to control it. They've brought the patient to the tower.'

Mei frowned. It was just after six in the morning; what time did the lifeguards start work?

'On our way,' she said as she flicked the switch for lights and sirens and Alex swung the ambulance in a one-hundred-and-eighty-degree turn and headed for the famous beach.

The streets had been decorated in preparation for Christmas. Somewhere in the past twenty-four hours the shops and restaurants seemed to have mutually decided to launch into the festive spirit. Decorations hung from the light poles and even their ambulance had a Christmas bauble hanging from the rear vision mirror. Mei loved Christmas but it did seem to arrive earlier every year. She supposed her parents would soon be digging out the decorations for the restaurant and she and

An Na would be busy stringing lights and tinsel. She wondered if Jet loved Christmas.

Perhaps he would be at the tower. 'What time do the lifeguards start work?' she asked.

'Six a.m. And they're on duty until seven at night.'

She hadn't realised they started that early. She'd been preparing herself to see Jet again next week, when she was back on day shift. What if he was on duty today? She wasn't mentally ready for this. It was only two days since she'd seen him on the beach at Paul's emergency and she hadn't anticipated seeing him again so soon.

She took a deep breath and told herself to relax. Maybe he wasn't rostered on. Maybe she was stressing over nothing.

But of course he was the lifeguard who greeted them at the door to the tower.

Her heart was racing. She was glad she was short; that way she didn't need to look him in the eye but instead she was face to face with his bare chest. Yet again. Didn't the man own a shirt?

She looked past him, trying to ignore the fact he was tall, lean, golden and glorious.

She didn't want to think of him that way. She didn't want to think of him at all.

But her head had been full of memories for the better part of the past two days and she was struggling to think about anything else.

She tensed as Jet greeted Alex. She had no cap or sunglasses to hide behind today, but maybe he still hadn't recognised her? Maybe he hadn't remembered her? Maybe she was getting herself all worked up over nothing.

'Hello, Mei.'

So he remembered her. That pleased her, appealed to the little bit of vanity she had, but she wished it didn't. It didn't make the situation any easier. Any less complicated. She was equal parts flattered that he hadn't forgotten her and annoyed with herself that she cared, but right now she needed to ignore both those feelings and get to work.

Would she be able to work with him? It was obvious it was going to be a regular occurrence. She'd have to find a way. She had a job to do. She had to focus on her job. On her patient. Their patient.

'Hello, Jet.'

Her voice was husky and she fought the

urge to clear her throat, knowing that would just draw attention to her flustered state. She brushed past him as she stepped inside the tower, aiming for nonchalance, hoping not to let him see how much he affected her and eager to get on with treating her patient, eager to have something else to focus on.

A treatment plinth was tucked against the wall in the lower section of the tower. A dark-haired woman with a pale face lay on the bed. Her skin was grey and covered with a sheen of sweat. She clutched a small green whistle in her hand and as Mei watched she put it in her mouth and sucked on it like a lollipop, seeking the pain relief from the drugs it administered.

'Hello, I'm Mei,' she said as she put her medical bag on the floor beside the bed, taking care not to knock the woman. 'I'm with the ambulance.'

Mei had hoped that treating the patient would have focused her attention, but Jet stood beside her as she introduced herself to the patient, giving her no space to gather her thoughts.

'Amandine is from France.' Mei could feel Jet's warm breath on her neck as he spoke.

'Do you speak English?' Mei asked.

The woman nodded but did not let go of the green whistle. Mei knew she was in pain and would find talking difficult, so she wasn't surprised when Jet stepped in to provide the history of the injury. 'She's got a nasty gash in her thigh. It's pretty deep and we had trouble stemming the bleeding.'

Someone had put a blanket over Amandine's torso but her legs were bare. Mei could see a tourniquet around Amandine's thigh, above the bandage. Blood had soaked through the layers, staining the fabric red. That didn't look good.

'This was a surfing accident?' Mei looked up at Jet, forgetting in her confusion that she was trying to avoid eye contact, but she couldn't figure out how Amandine could have cut her leg so badly while surfing.

Jet nodded. 'The fin on another surfer's board cut across her thigh.'

'The fin on a surfboard did that?' Mei hadn't realised they were sharp enough to cut skin and, by the sound of Jet's description, right through the skin and into the muscle. But hopefully the sharpness would at least mean they would be dealing with a neat wound with no jagged edges. Mei wondered if she should take a look at the wound. Would it be better just to transport Amandine to hospital? What if it wasn't as bad as the lifeguards thought? She didn't want to make a drama, but there was no reason to doubt them. They had seen the wound, dressed it, and it was still bleeding. She must attempt to stem the bleeding before moving the patient.

'Is it all right if I take a look?' She needed to know what they were dealing with. Could they move her safely or was that likely to cause more bleeding? How much blood had she already lost?

Amandine nodded but it was obvious she was feeling uncomfortable. That made two of them, Mei thought.

The tower was crowded. Every square inch of space had a purpose and there wasn't much room around the bed. Jet was on Mei's right, standing close, filling the space. He was close enough that she could feel his body heat and his proximity made the skin on her forearms tingle.

He smelt of the ocean. Of salt and sun.

He smelt the same as he had eight years ago.

Mei wondered if she could give Jet a job to do, something to get him to move out of her space.

'Alex, can you give me a hand?' She'd replace Jet with Alex, she decided. Together they'd have a look at Amandine's wound. Alex moved in as she pulled on a pair of gloves, but Jet only moved to Mei's left.

He brushed past her, his leg grazing her bottom as he squeezed behind her. Mei's hands trembled as she unwrapped the bandages to examine Amandine's injury. She took a deep breath to focus her mind as Jet kept up a conversation with their patient.

'Is this your first time in Australia?'

'*Oui*, I arrived yesterday.'

Jet continued chatting to Amandine and Mei knew he was distracting her deliberately, giving her something other than her injury to focus on.

She was well aware that Amandine's eyes

were fixed on Jet, that she couldn't care less what Mei and Alex were doing. Which was just as well. Her leg was a mess. Mei kept her eyes fixed on her patient. She couldn't afford to be distracted by Jet's voice as well.

Amandine had sustained a nasty injury. The gash in her thigh was deep into the muscle. She needed to go to hospital and would probably need the skills of a plastic surgeon. Luckily, the fin of the surfboard appeared to have missed all major arteries, but she would have a nasty scar as a reminder of her holiday in Australia.

Mei cleaned the wound and did her best to hold the edges together with butterfly strips before rewrapping Amandine's thigh with fresh sterile bandages.

'You'll need to come with us to the hospital,' she told Amandine. There was nothing more they could do for her here in the lifeguard tower. They needed to get going. *She* needed to get going.

'I'll get the stretcher,' Alex said, and he ducked out of the tower before Mei had a chance to respond.

Mei gave Amandine an injection for the

pain and then finished bandaging her thigh. She looked around, wondering how they were going to get the stretcher into the tower. She knew it wasn't going to fit easily and there was no way Amandine could walk out of there on her injured leg or after sucking on the green whistle.

'The stretcher's not going to fit in here,' she said as she taped the bandage in place and began to repack the kit, looking for tasks to keep her hands and mind busy.

'I've got this,' Jet said as the tower door opened, announcing Alex's return. 'Keep sucking on the whistle, Amandine, while that injection takes effect. I'm going to carry you to the stretcher,' he said and, before Mei could ask what he was doing, and before she had time to wonder if it was safe, Jet had slid one arm under Amandine's thighs, another around her back and she was clinging to him with her free hand as he scooped her up.

Mei stepped back, out of the way as Jet spun on his heel and carried Amandine out of the tower. And then she forgot to move. She stood, rooted to the spot, transfixed by the sight of Jet effortlessly lifting this woman.

Amandine wasn't a big girl, but she wasn't tiny either, and while Jet's muscles bulged he didn't appear to be struggling.

As Jet gently lowered the patient onto the ambulance stretcher Mei finally got her feet moving just in time to see Amandine gazing adoringly at Jet. The effects of the green whistle often induced a feeling of euphoria and Amandine was no exception. She had completely forgotten about her pain, probably due to a combination of the pain relief and being in Jet's arms, and Mei couldn't blame her. Jet was gorgeous.

Alex strapped Amandine onto the stretcher as Mei dumped the medical kit at her feet and released the brakes, in a hurry now to get away from the beach. She knew she wouldn't be able to think straight until she put some distance between herself and Jet. Between herself and his golden gorgeousness. Between herself and the sight of his tanned perfection and blue eyes.

Mei pushed the stretcher to the ambulance and Jet followed behind her. She locked the stretcher into the rails and pushed the button to load it into the ambulance before climbing into the back with her patient. She turned her head, waiting for Alex to close the doors, but Jet was there instead.

He smiled and winked at her as he pushed the rear doors shut and Mei could feel a blush staining her cheeks. He hadn't said anything, thank God, as Mei knew she wouldn't have been able to formulate a sensible response; her brain felt like scrambled noodles.

She needed to get herself together. She needed to work out a plan. A strategy.

The sun was well and truly up over the horizon by the time Mei and Alex handed Amandine over to the hospital staff and returned to the station to knock off. Mei was eager to get home in time to take An Na to school. Normally after a night shift she would then go home and sleep for a few hours, but she was far too wound up. She messaged her sister-in-law, desperate to meet for a coffee after school drop-off.

Somehow she got An Na organised and to school. Thank God, at the age of seven, her daughter was too engrossed in the day ahead to notice her mother's distracted air.

Mei arrived first. The café was playing

Christmas carols and listening to songs about sleigh rides in the snow when the Australian sun was high overhead and it was almost thirty degrees Celsius at ten in the morning always made Mei smile. It was quite incongruous, but it didn't diminish the excitement that started to build in her at this time of year. She loved Christmas, loved the time spent with her family, loved the traditions her family celebrated. When her family had moved to Australia from Hong Kong her parents had combined the more formal British and Chinese Christmas traditions with the laid-back Australian style and Mei loved the uniqueness of their celebrations.

She hummed along to the music while she scrolled through photos of An Na on her phone and waited for Su-Lin. She noted some similarities between An Na and Jet that she'd forgotten about. They had more in common than just their smile. The tilt of An Na's head when she was deep in thought and her long fingers had been inherited from her father, but Mei wasn't certain she wanted to see the similarities.

She put her phone away as her sister-in-law arrived, pushing a pram; Mei's nephew was fast asleep.

'What's the emergency?' Su-Lin asked as she parked the pram beside the table.

'Thanks for coming,' Mei said. 'I hope I haven't interrupted your day.'

'You have—' Su-Lin laughed '—but I'm glad of the interruption. I could murder another coffee. I feel like I've done a day's work already. I had to get Dan to daycare, Vivian to school and Kai has got his vaccinations today, but I'm guessing, given that you're still in your uniform, that I'm not going to get much sympathy from you. I have no idea how I'm going to manage when I go back to work. Three kids are *so* much more work than two.'

'I thought you were going to have help?' Mei asked. Su-Lin was on maternity leave from her job as a lawyer and Mei's brother was a dentist. They could afford help.

'Bo wants me to find a nanny—it would make sense, rather than paying for two lots of childcare—but I haven't started looking yet.'

Mei had always thought her brother and

sister-in-law's life looked easy in comparison to her own. They had plenty of money and there were two of them to raise the kids. She wasn't jealous but envious. She knew she was lucky to have not only their help but that of her parents, but she still dreamt of being independent. She could move out of her parents' apartment, but she told herself they would miss An Na. Even though she knew she stayed put because it was easier for her. She didn't see the point in disrupting everyone's lives just to make her own harder.

'How much longer until you go back to work?' she asked.

'A couple of months. February,' Su-Lin said as Kai woke from his nap and started gurgling in his pram.

Mei picked him up, keen to have a cuddle.

'You need to have more kids,' Su-Lin told her.

'You just said how hard it is!'

'You don't have to have lots, just one more. Babies suit you.'

'I do adore babies,' she admitted. She loved their smell, their softness. She loved imagining the possibilities for them. She would actually love to do it all over again, but she had promised herself she'd do it differently next time. For a start she'd plan the pregnancy. She didn't want another surprise; she wanted to enjoy the excitement, the anticipation, and not be terrified of the future. She wanted a partner to support her, she wanted to get some sleep and enjoy being a mother.

She knew some of her fears would ease the second time around, although she suspected she would always be scared of failing in her parenting duties somehow. It was a constant worry, probably heightened by the fact that, for An Na, she was it. But having a partner might help to allay some of that fear. It would have to, surely?

'An Na is old enough now,' Su-Lin said. 'You should start dating. We need to find you a man.'

'That's what I needed to see you about.'

'What? Really? Have you met someone?' Su-Lin clapped her hands in excitement.

'No. It's not that,' Mei said. 'I wanted to talk to you about An Na's father.'

'The surfer?'

Mei nodded. Su-Lin knew all about Jet.

Su-Lin had married Mei's brother, but their families had been connected since they were babies. Both Mei's parents and Su-Lin's had emigrated from Hong Kong to Australia when Mei was only two years old. Su-Lin had been like an older sister to her and she was the one Mei had turned to when she'd discovered she was pregnant.

When it had been too late for a termination and Mei was beside herself, worried about her parents' reaction and knowing she couldn't possibly manage seven years of med school with a baby, she had turned to Su-Lin. She'd been terrified that she wouldn't cope, that she'd ruin not only her own life but her child's as well. But Su-Lin and Mei's brother, Bo, had been supportive and had certainly helped to smooth over what could only be described as a rocky patch in Mei's life and also in her relationship with her parents. She knew they'd been disappointed in her, she'd been disappointed in herself, but they had crossed that bridge and ever since they had been an amazing support for her and for An Na.

It had taken them all a while to get to

where they were now. For Mei to stop feeling ashamed that she'd put herself in this position and that she couldn't manage on her own. For her to accept her parents' help without feeling guilty. For a long time she'd felt she'd let everyone down, but now they had their routine, their roles and An Na was loved and supported by her extended family.

Su-Lin had been the one who had gone back to Byron Bay with Mei in search of Jet eight years ago. She had comforted her when they hadn't been able to find him. She and Bo had supported her when she'd told her parents about her pregnancy. She'd been with her when An Na was born and she'd been beside her every step of the way since. Su-Lin was her best friend and had always given her unwavering support and sage advice and she needed her wisdom and practical advice again now.

How would Jet fit into the roles they had all adopted for themselves? How would his presence change the dynamic? How would his presence affect An Na? And Mei?

What if he didn't like the way she'd brought up their child? It hadn't been his fault that he wasn't around, no matter how irritated Mei had been at times that he hadn't been there to help. What if he was critical of her parenting skills? She was just beginning to feel that she knew what she was doing after all these years. What if he found fault?

She had a thousand questions and she needed Su-Lin to help her make sense of it all.

'What about him?' Su-Lin asked.

'He's here. In Bondi.'

'You've seen him?'

Mei nodded.

'Where?'

'At work.'

'He's a paramedic?'

'No.'

'A patient?'

'No.'

'A policeman?'

'No,' Mei huffed. 'If you let me finish, I'll tell you,' she said. 'He's a lifeguard on Bondi Beach.'

'A lifeguard! How long has he been here?'

'I have no idea. I didn't get a chance to find out.' She didn't admit she hadn't tried.

'And does he know about An Na? Have you told him?'

'Not yet.'

'You will tell him?'

'I'll have to.'

'How did you feel, seeing him again?'

Conflicted. She couldn't deny that she was still attracted to him, that she was still drawn to him. That had surprised her. She had never reacted like that to anyone else— that strong sense of fate, inevitability. She was trying to put that to one side; there were more important issues than her hormones.

But how did she put her feelings into words?

Despite wanting Su-Lin's advice, she knew she couldn't tell her how she really felt. She didn't need advice about her emotions. She needed practical advice.

'I'm not sure how I feel,' she admitted. 'I've spent so many years being angry with him…' That was true but, seeing him again, that anger had diminished. It was still there but it wasn't as overwhelming, as all-encompassing. Anger and irritation had been moved aside to make room for a host of other emotions. Seeing him, hearing his voice and feeling his fingers brush her skin had made her feel alive, afraid and apprehensive. Anxious and excited.

'You're still angry with him? After eight years?'

Mei nodded.

'How is that even possible?' Su-Lin wanted to know.

'Because every time I have a bad day—when An Na was not sleeping, or not feeding, or teething, or crying because she didn't want to go to daycare, I would imagine Jet, somewhere in the great big world, surfing, dancing, having fun. In my mind he had no responsibilities, he was out there enjoying his life and that would annoy me. I never wanted to give An Na up but I resented the fact that I was raising her on my own.'

'To be fair, he didn't know about her.'

'I realise that. I know I'm being unreasonable, but it's how I felt. How I feel. All this time he's been right here in Sydney, living his life, while I've been raising An Na. He got to chase his dreams, while I had to give mine up.'

'You can't blame him for things he's known nothing about. Was it his dream to become a lifeguard? I thought he was going to travel the world and try to make it as a professional surfer?'

Mei nodded. 'He did want to be a professional surfer. At the time I thought that sounded romantic and exciting and adventurous. Once I had An Na I thought it just sounded unrealistic.'

'So, while you're angry at him, you don't actually know how his life has turned out. You don't know what has happened to him over the past eight years. What has happened to his dream. It's probably fair to say that being a lifeguard wasn't his dream. Maybe this is your chance to sort things out. To forgive, in a sense. To move on and make a fresh start. You need to talk to him.'

'I know. I will. I just need to work out how and when.' She was incredibly nervous about what would happen next.

'Is he married?'

'I have no idea,' she said as a realisation hit her. 'What if he is? What if he wants to take her?'

'He can't just take her.'

'Oh, God, what a mess.' Mei put her head in her hands. 'This could get complicated.'

'Don't start worrying about things that might not happen. We'll work this out. You liked him once; I'm sure he's still a decent guy.'

'Do you think I should get a family lawyer?' Mei asked, completely ignoring Su-Lin's advice about not stressing over things she couldn't control or that hadn't happened yet.

'I don't think that's necessary at this stage, but family law isn't my area of expertise.' Su-Lin worked as in-house counsel for a large bank. 'If you like, I can ask a friend who is a family lawyer. I'll see if she is free over the weekend and if she minds if you pick her brains. We've got a dinner to go to on Friday, but we'll be home on Saturday. I could ask her over then.'

'Saturday is no good; it's the ambulance Christmas party. I've said I'll go. It's a good chance to meet all my new colleagues.'

'You're going to a party?'

'You don't need to sound quite so surprised.'

'Why not? This is a big deal for you. What are you going to wear?'

'I haven't thought about it.'

'Just make sure it's something other than your paramedic's uniform or jeans.'

'I have absolutely nothing else in my wardrobe.'

'You know you're welcome to borrow something of mine.'

'Your clothes are far too glamorous for me.' Su-Lin's wardrobe was extensive and she was always immaculately dressed. Even today, when all she was doing was running errands, she looked as if she had stepped off a catwalk, but Mei had long since given up comparing her style to Su-Lin's. She knew they were chalk and cheese.

'Don't be ridiculous. I've got a red dress that will look gorgeous on you and perfect for a Christmas party. Why don't Vivian and I pick An Na up on Saturday and bring the dress over and help you get ready? An Na and Vivian would love to see you getting dressed up. And then we'll take An Na home with us; she can spend the night.'

Mei knew she'd accept Su-Lin's offer of a sleepover. She knew how much An Na loved spending time with her cousins, plus it would give Mei a chance to sleep in.

'And that way,' Su-Lin continued with a smile, 'if you meet someone nice, you don't need to rush home. You don't need to come home at all.'

'It's a work show,' Mei protested. 'I'm not about to hook up with one of my colleagues!' Her days of reckless behaviour were well and truly behind her. She had other responsibilities now but, even if she didn't, one big mistake was all she was prepared to make in her lifetime. 'I'm quite happy with my life.'

'It's not you I'm thinking of,' Su-Lin said. 'It really is time you started dating. An Na needs a father figure and your parents expect you to get married.'

Mei knew her parents wanted her married. The fact that she'd had an unplanned pregnancy and was now a single mother was a source of disappointment to them. She was disappointed in herself—not because she was a mother but because her mistake had cost her her dream of becoming a doctor. It was her only regret, but one she'd learned to live with. It would have been impossible to manage; she wouldn't have had the time or energy to cope. Something would have failed, she would have failed, either at being a doctor or being a mother, and that was a risk she hadn't been prepared to take.

She was only just coping now with raising a child and working and that was with the help of her extended family.

'I don't have time to date,' she told Su-Lin.

Mei had never really dated anyone seriously despite her sister-in-law's best efforts at matchmaking and she'd always been adamant that she was happy alone. But she knew that wasn't true. She wanted a relationship, someone to share her life with, but she was terrified of mucking things up, of not choosing wisely.

She'd worked hard to make a happy, uncomplicated life for An Na and she was trying not to put unrealistic expectations on her. She understood why her parents had raised her and her brother the way they had, but she wanted her daughter to live a more care-free childhood and Mei didn't want any of the dramas that could come with failed relationships. An Na had good male role models in her grandfather and uncle; her life wasn't lacking but Mei's was. But she didn't want to risk failure.

'I'd need some sort of guarantee that it was going to work out before I expend precious energy on dating.'

'That's ridiculous,' Su-Lin protested. 'You can't know in advance. You have to give someone a try.'

But Mei wanted—needed—a guarantee next time. She'd given her heart to Jet, unintentionally; she hadn't meant to fall so hard for him, a holiday fling. She'd known it would never work—he was a young man with no bigger goals than to travel the world. He was headed for the surf breaks of Hawaii, and she was headed for med school—but that hadn't stopped her from falling for him.

They'd had instant chemistry, but that wasn't what she'd fallen for. She'd fallen for his soft heart and the loneliness that lay beneath a veneer of confidence. The loneliness that mirrored her own. She'd known he'd needed her and she was happy to give herself over. She hadn't expected not to get all of herself back though. But that was exactly what happened. She'd taken a piece of him with her when she'd returned to Sydney but left a piece of her heart behind.

Next time she gave her heart away she needed a guarantee that it wasn't going to hurt. Next time she gave her heart away it was going to be to her true love.

CHAPTER THREE

MEI READJUSTED THE straps on her borrowed dress, checking that she was still decent. Su-Lin's idea of a party dress revealed a little more cleavage than Mei was comfortable with, but she had nothing else to wear. Her wardrobe consisted of jeans, T-shirts and her uniform and she had to admit Su-Lin had been right; red suited her and it did feel good to dress up for a change. She'd even relented and let Su-Lin do her make-up. While it could still only be called minimal it was more than she normally wore. Her job as a paramedic was far from glamorous whereas Su-Lin, as a corporate lawyer, was a dab hand at applying make-up and had transformed Mei's look from tired, suburban single mum to a festive twenty-something. On the outside at least.

Satisfied that all her parts were where they were supposed to be, she climbed the stairs to the Bondi Pavilion. She wasn't nervous. She was used to making conversation and, being a work party, she would have something in common with everyone here, but it had been a long time since she'd gone to a function on her own. Since she'd gone to a function at all.

The sound of live music greeted her as she pushed open the door. She ducked under some low-hanging mistletoe and looked around the room. Christmas lights and decorations were strung around the room and a band was set up on a stage in the opposite corner. There was already a crowd on the small dance floor and the room seemed to be bursting with people. Surely they couldn't all be from the Bondi Ambulance Station? Perhaps a few stations had combined their celebrations.

She spotted some of the paramedics she'd shared shifts with standing in a group near the stage and headed in their direction. She'd start with Alex and Poppy, two familiar faces; there'd be time to meet new people later.

'Hello, Alex. Poppy.'

'Mei! Hi,' Poppy greeted her. 'You look great; that's a fabulous dress.'

Mei squirmed under the compliment, aware that it drew everyone's attention to her. She preferred to fly under the radar. 'Thank you,' she managed to reply as she resisted the urge to check that everything was in the right place yet again.

The lifeguard who had driven her to the resuscitation job was standing beside Poppy. His name popped into her head as she wondered what he was doing there.

'Hello, Ryder,' she said. She would have loved to have a quick glance around to see if there were other lifeguards at the party, to see if Jet was there, but her back was to the room. She didn't turn; she wasn't sure if she wanted to see Jet or not. Equal parts yes and no.

'You've met?' Poppy asked.

Mei nodded. 'We met at the beach, on a job.'

Poppy tucked her arm through Ryder's.

'He's my fiancé.' She was looking at Ryder as she said, 'I still can't get used to the idea that we're getting married.'

'Congratulations.' Mei relaxed. Ryder was there with Poppy. She wouldn't be bumping into Jet. 'When is the wedding?'

'We're not sure yet,' Poppy said.

Ryder answered at the same time, 'I'm thinking March.'

'You are?' Poppy sounded surprised. 'March?'

Ryder nodded and kissed Poppy. 'I'd marry you tomorrow if I could. I don't see any reason to have a long engagement.'

Poppy looked very much like a woman in love as she beamed at Ryder before she turned back to Mei, who was beginning to feel a little as if she was intruding on something private, despite the fact that Alex was also still standing there.

'Are you married? Dating?' Poppy asked Mei.

'Stop it,' Ryder said.

'What?'

'You're doing the thing that all couples do—trying to set everyone else up.'

'It's fine,' Mei said. 'I'm single but I'm not looking to be set up. I've got too much on my plate at the moment with the new job and all.'

'Well. If you change your mind, Ryder knows plenty of eligible men. Half the lifeguards are single. He can introduce you to some tonight if you want.'

'Tonight?' Mei looked around the room, suddenly nervous.

'Yes. The lifeguards are here too. The party is for all the Bondi first responders and emergency services—the firies, police, paramedics and lifeguards, because we all work so closely together it's become an annual tradition to celebrate together.'

'I hadn't realised that the party was for everyone,' Mei replied. Her heart was racing at the thought that Jet could be here too.

'Christmas is a crazy time in Bondi,' Alex added. 'So we have to celebrate early—we'll be working flat out for the next month, right up past New Year's Day.'

Ryder was looking at his empty glass. 'I need a beer and you need a drink, Mei. What can I get you? Champagne? Wine?'

Mei wasn't much of a drinker, alcohol

tended to go straight to her head, but it was Christmas. One champagne couldn't hurt. 'I'd love a champagne, thanks.' The idea that Jet might be at the party had made her jittery; perhaps a drink would help to calm her nerves.

'Alex, do you need another?'

Alex checked his drink and drained the last mouthful. 'I'll come with you.'

The men headed for the bar, leaving Poppy and Mei alone.

'How are you settling in at the station?' Poppy asked.

'Good. Apart from the sand. I swear I empty half the beach from my boots every night. I hadn't realised how often we'd be called to the beach.'

'It does keep us busy, especially at this time of year. There can be forty thousand people at Bondi on a summer's day, that's the population of a large country town, so there's plenty for us to do there. Where were you working before?'

'In Western Sydney, but this is closer to home. I've been applying for a transfer for ages, but I've only got a few years' experience and I kept missing out to more qualified paramedics. How long have you been at the station?'

'Only a couple of months.'

Mei smiled. 'So, you're one of the ones I was competing against. Where did you move from?'

'Brisbane.'

'Did you move with Ryder?'

'No, we grew up together but we hadn't seen each other for twelve years. I bumped into him again here.' Poppy looked past Mei towards the bar and smiled. Mei didn't turn her head, but she could tell from Poppy's dreamy expression that she was looking at Ryder. 'I can't believe we're getting married.'

'That's twice you've said that. Don't you want to get married?'

'Funnily enough, I do, but I never expected that I would. I didn't grow up in a traditional family so this is a big deal for me.'

'Where did you grow up? Brisbane?'

'No, I grew up in Byron Bay.'

Mei's heart thudded in her chest at Poppy's mention of Byron Bay. She'd been thinking about Byron often over the past week but to hear someone else mention it, to hear she had lived there, was a little surreal.

'I grew up with Ryder. He was a friend of my brother's,' Poppy was saying and Mei forced herself to focus. 'Speaking of the devil, here he comes.'

Poppy was looking over Mei's shoulder and this time Mei turned to see who was in her field of vision. And then immediately wished she hadn't.

Jet was walking towards them.

'Jet is your *brother*?'

She hoped Poppy was going to say no even while she knew it was inevitable that the two of them were related. Seeing them together, both tall, blonde, tanned and gorgeous, it was obvious they were related.

'You know Jet?'

Surprise made Mei incapable of stringing two words together and when she nodded in reply, Poppy concluded, 'Of course, you would have met him at work. Yep, he's my big brother.'

Mei took a deep breath as she tried to quell the rising panic. She had an overwhelming sense that she wasn't keeping up, that things were spiralling out of her control. She hadn't been able to decide if she wanted Jet to be here tonight or not, and now he was walking towards her and she was totally unprepared.

She knew she wouldn't be able to avoid him for ever, but she wasn't ready. In a social setting there was no easy way to escape. At work she could avoid difficult conversations and she always had an out—at some point she always needed to get back into the ambulance and leave the beach. She could leave the party but she hadn't been there long and her intention had been to socialise with her new colleagues. She wasn't going to let Jet scare her off.

He was smiling as he came towards them, fixing Mei to the spot as she got a glimpse of An Na. She let her eyes run over him, wanting, needing to avoid getting entranced by his beautiful face. He was wearing light-weight trousers and a blue shirt that matched the colour of his eyes. The shirt was decorated with surfing Santas and his outfit made her smile.

Too late, she realised he would think she was smiling at him. For him.

'Hello, Mei. Ryder sent me over with drinks for you both.'

Mei hadn't noticed that he was carrying two champagne flutes and what appeared to be a water. She had been far too immersed in his eyes.

'Is the water for me?' Poppy asked.

'No, it's mine. Why?'

'I'm not drinking. I have to work tomorrow.'

'You'd better check with Ryder. I don't think he got that memo.' Jet grinned as Poppy excused herself.

'And then there were two,' he said, still smiling, as he held out a glass to Mei. 'Champagne?'

'Thank you.' Mei took the glass Jet offered. 'You did that on purpose,' she said as she tried, unsuccessfully, to ignore the heat that spread through her as Jet's fingers brushed hers.

'Did what?'

'Brought Poppy the wrong drink.'

'And why would I have done that?' His smile widened and Mei's knees wobbled.

Mei didn't answer. She'd imagined it was

his ploy to get her to himself but she couldn't say that. At best, she might be wrong; at worst, it would make her look conceited.

'Would it be so that I could speak to you alone, without my sister around?' he asked.

Perhaps it had nothing to do with wanting time alone with her but simply a desire to keep Poppy in the dark about how they knew each other. She hadn't thought about that.

She sipped her champagne, using it as an excuse to avoid answering his question as she cautioned herself to relax. She realised her insecurities were carrying her away. She didn't need to try to work out what he was thinking—more than likely he wasn't think-ing anything at all—and he certainly would have no idea about the thoughts in her head, the ones that were threatening to drive her crazy. She would relax and try to pretend that he was just a casual acquaintance and not a man who could send her hormones wild and make her go from annoyed to weak at the knees with just one smile or the brief-est touch of his hand. She'd pretend he was a casual acquaintance and not the father of her child.

'You look worried,' he said. 'I won't tell anyone about our wild weekend if that's what's concerning you.'

Shit, maybe he could read her mind! But that wasn't what she was worried about. Well, not the only thing. Jet could promise to keep it a secret but what he didn't realise was that everyone was going to find out about their history anyway. She couldn't keep An Na a secret for ever. What *she* hadn't counted on was that 'everyone' included Jet's sister, which meant that her new colleagues would also be privy to that history. Would they judge her harshly?

'I'm not worried,' she lied. She wasn't only worried—she was nervous too. But it wasn't their history making her skittish, it was Jet. The way she felt around him unsettled her. The moment she saw him she forgot to be angry. She forgot about all the years when she'd been literally left holding the baby and all she could think about was how she'd felt when he'd held her in his arms, when he'd kissed her, when he'd made love to her. She could feel a blush start to rise in her cheeks and was grateful that the room was only lit by strings of Christmas lights.

'Catch me up,' he said.

That might have been possible if it hadn't been years since they'd seen each other. If her whole life hadn't changed. 'On the last eight years?'

'Is that how long it's been?'

'Almost to the day.'

He was still smiling as he said, 'You must have lots to tell me then.'

If he only knew.

'You're not married, are you?' he asked and before she could respond he had reached for her left hand, holding her fingers gently in his and turned her hand over, looking for a ring.

His thumb brushed her knuckles and her hand trembled as heat raced up her arm and filled her chest. Her heart was pounding as she shook her head. 'No, never married.'

She wondered what he'd say if she said she had a daughter. She was tempted to see what sort of reaction she would get but she knew that was irrelevant—she was going to have to tell him at some point, but she wanted to find out what sort of man he'd become first. How his life had turned out. What would she be dealing with? What if he had other children? What if An Na had siblings? If he had a family, would they accept An Na?

Did he have a wife? A girlfriend? Who would Mei be competing with?

Where had that thought come from? She knew she was getting carried away. Creating issues before she knew what the situation was. She needed to slow down. 'What about you? Married? Kids?' she asked.

He laughed. 'No, that's not on my agenda.'

He was two years older than her, which would make him twenty-eight, or maybe twenty-nine now. She was partly relieved to hear that the added complication of Jet having a wife and kids didn't exist but then she wondered if he'd ever want to get married. If he'd ever want a family.

He had a mischievous gleam in his eye as he asked, 'So, are you still behaving scandalously?'

'No!' She withdrew her hand from Jet's hold.

'That's too bad.'

She recalled his devil-may-care attitude. Rules and conventions didn't faze him, and while she couldn't imagine behaving scandalously again—she had certainly paid a price for that last time—she did wish she'd retained a little of the spontaneity that she'd found in Byron Bay, a little of the spark that Jet had brought out in her. But she knew that had been lost under the weight of responsibility and parenthood.

'What we did, what *I* did, was completely out of character for me. I *never* would have done that if I were in Sydney.'

'Why not?'

'I was too afraid of what people who knew me might say.'

'What did your girlfriends say? They were with you in Byron that weekend.'

'They were far too busy having their own adventures, celebrating the end of our school days and the start of their freedom, to worry about me.' She'd lost touch with those friends over the course of the next few months. An unexpected teenage pregnancy had been a sure way of sending her on a different trajectory to her peers and her embarrassment had ensured that she'd deliberately cut those ties.

'You know,' he said, 'I wasn't sure it was you, that first time I saw you on Bondi.'

'No?'

He shook his head. 'You looked familiar but beneath your cap and sunglasses it was hard to be certain. And you said you were going to study medicine. I wasn't expecting to see you working as a paramedic. I thought you had planned to be a doctor.'

'My plans changed,' Mei responded. 'I thought *you* were going to travel the world and live the life of a professional surfer.'

'My plans changed too,' he said. He looked away, but not before Mei had seen the shadow that crossed behind his eyes. What had caused that? Had she offended him?

She immediately wondered if she should apologise. Not that she was sure what for, but that was a habit of hers. She spent her life feeling pressured to live up to certain expectations and then apologising if she didn't meet them and that impulse spilled over into other aspects of her life. But before she could say sorry or ask him what was wrong he changed the subject.

'Do you like being a paramedic?'

She sipped her champagne as she considered her answer. 'I enjoy the fact that every day is different and that I'm helping people, but I still wish I was a doctor.'

'What's stopping you?'

'So many things,' she sighed. She had never let go of the idea of becoming a doctor, but the dream had faded as the reality of life took over until, eventually, she'd had to let it go.

'Regrets?'

She nodded. 'Some,' she said honestly. 'What about you?'

'Regrets? I've had a few...but then again—' he laughed '—I don't want to talk about regrets.'

'No?'

'No.' He was watching her closely now, his blue eyes intent on her face. They were standing close together, the volume of the band made it impossible to hold a conversation at a distance, but Jet stepped even closer. He bent his head until his lips almost brushed her ear and his voice was low and soft as he said, 'I want to dance. With you.'

She remembered how well he could dance. Mei had spent years in ballet class, dancing was something she loved, and Jet's dancing ability had been one of the many things that had attracted her to him. He was light on his feet, balanced. He had good rhythm and enjoyed dancing almost as much as she did.

He enjoyed dancing almost as much as he enjoyed sex.

She knew it was dangerous to accept. She knew she should say no, but no words came out of her mouth.

He took her drink and then he took her hand.

She hadn't said she'd dance with him. She hadn't needed to. They both knew she would.

The song ended and the band started a slower number but still she let him lead her to the dance floor.

Jet was well over six feet tall and he towered over her. Mei was only five feet four inches tall, and even with heels on she was little, but she didn't feel insignificant as she stepped into his hold. She felt delicate, but safe. She felt precious.

She closed her eyes and the years fell away as the music took her back to the night when they'd first met. It was almost as though she could feel the sand of Byron Bay between her toes.

She remembered how it felt to be in his arms, both dancing on the sand and in his bed. Whoever had coined the phrase about dancing leading to sex had got it right as far as she and Jet were concerned. Dancing with Jet on the beach had led her down the path towards her future.

Their first dance had been around a bonfire on the beach. She'd been with her group of girlfriends when she'd seen him, dancing on the opposite side of the fire. He'd been hard to miss. Tall and blond, he'd glowed in the firelight; his white gold hair had caught the glow of the flames, shining like a beacon against the black darkness of the night.

He'd locked eyes with Mei and he'd moved around the fire and joined the circle of girls. He'd danced with them all as a group until, at some point, it had become just the two of them together. Still separate, not touching, but definitely dancing as a couple.

And then she'd been in his arms. She'd been attracted to him immediately but once he'd held her in his arms she was done for. That was all it had taken. That was when she'd known she would sleep with him.

And then they hadn't been dancing at all. He'd bent his head and kissed her, brushing his lips over hers, and she'd lost her mind. Her feet had stopped moving but her knees wobbled. He'd held her up, supported her as she kissed him back.

She hadn't even known his name at that point.

She'd let him take her hand and lead her to a blanket on the sand. They'd listened to the music and kissed until the fire was just glowing embers.

At some point her girlfriends had told her they were going home to bed. They hadn't wanted to leave her with a stranger, but he hadn't felt like a stranger by then.

She'd gone home with him just as the sky was beginning to lighten in the east.

Home was a caravan on a block of land

behind the beach. It was tiny but clean and had a bed just big enough for two.

She hadn't fallen in love. Not that night. It had been lust, pure and simple, and she'd made a conscious decision to give in to her desires. To give herself to Jet.

There had been no commitment, no promises, no expectations of anything other than fulfilling their desire.

She hadn't told him she was a virgin and he hadn't asked. She had danced for years, there'd been no pain, and he never suspected that he was her first lover.

He hadn't asked about contraception either and she hadn't thought to mention it.

That had been her only mistake.

If she'd known then what she did now, would she have danced with him at all?

She knew she would. She was doing exactly the same thing tonight, but this time she would be cautious. This time it would just be a dance. One dance where she could enjoy the feeling of being in his arms before she went home. It was highly likely that he was going to be a part of her life in some way, given he was the father of her child, but she couldn't let herself fall for him. They would always be connected but she didn't need to fall in love.

'Jet, you promised me a dance.'

Mei opened her eyes to find a pretty blonde woman standing beside her. It took her a minute to get her bearings, she'd been firmly lost in the past, but as the song ended and the tempo of the music changed she finally realised the woman was cutting in on her.

Jet looked as though he might be about to ask if she minded but she didn't have a monopoly on him and she knew the wisest course of action would be to put some distance between them.

'Thanks for the dance. I'm going to grab a drink,' she said before he had a chance to speak. She turned to the blonde, 'He's all yours.'

Giving him up willingly was one thing, watching him dancing with myriad other women was another thing altogether. Mei tried not to notice who he was dancing with, she tried to keep engaged with conversations with her colleagues, but it was impossible to ignore the fact that Jet had no shortage of partners on the dance floor. It wasn't surprising, a man who could dance was always going to have plenty of partners, but it made her wonder if that held true in all aspects of his life as well. She suspected it would. He exuded charm and confidence. He had grown into a man who was comfortable in his skin and that was a highly attractive trait. Combined with his physical attributes, she knew he would have no shortage of female attention and companionship.

Eight years had passed since they'd spent a weekend together. She'd slept with two men since. She knew her experience would be vastly inferior to Jet's and that put her at a disadvantage. She couldn't blame her inexperience on youth any more and watching him with other women, women who she assumed were vastly more confident and knowledgeable than her, convinced her that there was no way Jet would be remotely interested in her now.

It was probably just as well. She didn't need a playboy in her life.

Mei turned her back on the dance floor,

thinking perhaps out of sight out of mind would work, but as the music stopped and the band announced a break between sets she felt the air around her begin to hum with an invisible energy and she knew Jet was nearby.

His hand brushed her hip as he stopped beside her. She had no idea if his touch had been intentional or not and, while he didn't seem aware of the contact, her heart leapt a little inside her ribcage.

'That took longer than expected,' he said.

'What did?'

'Getting off the dance floor.'

She was pleased that he'd come straight back to her, that he'd chosen her company in preference to one of his other dance partners, but she was also a little annoyed that he'd waited until the music stopped. He didn't have to keep dancing.

Mei took a deep breath as she gathered her thoughts. Jet made her feel so conflicted, so nervous and anxious, annoyed and excited. He made her feel things she hadn't felt in years, things she didn't *want* to feel, and that irritated her.

She felt vulnerable and exposed. Over the

past few years she had learnt to be strong and independent and she didn't want someone else to influence her emotions or her character—especially not Jet. He'd had enough impact on her life.

'Will you dance with me again when the band come back on?' he asked.

Mei shook her head while she thought of an excuse. She couldn't afford to let her guard down…she couldn't afford to step back into his arms.

'No, I'm about to head home.'

'Already? The party's only just getting started.'

She knew that wasn't true, but it was also far from over and she couldn't stay. She needed to put some distance between them. 'I have to be up early in the morning.'

'Are you working?'

'No.'

'Then surely you can stay a little longer. Can't you sleep in tomorrow?'

She shook her head again and decided to test him. 'No. There's no sleeping in when you have a child.'

'A child?' She heard the surprise in his

voice and saw it on his face. She watched his expression and she could tell he was scrolling back through their earlier conversation, wondering if he'd asked that question and then realising he hadn't.

He'd asked if she was married. *She'd* asked if he had kids.

'You're a mother?'

She nodded. 'A single mother.'

She waited for him to ask if she had a son or a daughter. Then waited to see if he'd ask how old her child was and panicked that if he asked that question it would lead her into a conversation she hadn't prepared for. But she needn't have worried. He didn't ask anything more and he didn't try to convince her to stay.

'Okay, I get it,' he said.

He didn't physically step back but she could see in his eyes that her status as a single mother had doused any interest he might have had in her. Telling him she had a child had been a test and Jet had failed. That was fine, she told herself. At least she knew where she stood, but she was disappointed in him and annoyed with herself for caring.

Seeing him withdraw made her realise she had been entertaining ideas of a happily ever after for her and for An Na. She'd been hoping he would embrace his instant family, embrace his daughter, embrace her. She'd pictured them building a life together, but finding out he was no longer interested in getting to know her again because she had a child was deflating.

But she tried to convince herself it was far better to know that now, before she got even more caught up in her fantasies of a happily ever after. Before she made another mistake.

It was their mistake that got her pregnant, but it was her mistake for choosing to sleep with a man she'd only just met. A man she barely knew. At least knowing how he felt saved her from making the same mistake again.

She'd be fine. She and An Na didn't need Jet in their lives.

But, for the first time in years, when she crawled into bed in a dark and silent house, the other side of the bed seemed very empty and Mei was swamped with loneliness. If An Na had been home she would have sneaked in with her, but she knew it wasn't her daughter's company she was missing. It wasn't her daughter's warmth that she craved. It was Jet's.

CHAPTER FOUR

JET AVOIDED THE dance floor after Mei had gone. He didn't want to dance with someone who wasn't Mei. The party had lost its spark and his mood had soured since she'd left. He was restless, off-kilter. He didn't feel like celebrating but he didn't want to go home yet either. He didn't want to go home alone. Earlier in the evening he had been anticipating spending time with Mei, perhaps even going home with her at the end of the night. He hadn't anticipated she'd be going home to a family.

It shouldn't matter, he told himself. He'd barely thought about her for the past eight years, even if he'd thought about her plenty over the past few days, and he could put her out of his mind again. Maybe he'd find someone else to take home.

But as he looked around the room he realised there was no one else who captured his attention the way Mei did. He hadn't been able to take his eyes off her all those years ago and it had been the same tonight. She had mesmerised him with her symmetrical doll-like features and dark eyes that seemed to be able to read his thoughts. There was a strong connection between them; it had been there eight years ago and it was still there now. He was drawn to her and he was powerless to fight it. Not that he wanted to.

There was something about her that made him feel less alone in the world. He felt that, even without talking, she understood him. Normally he wasn't fussed about people being on his wavelength, understanding him; he was quite happy as a solitary man and if he wanted a female opinion or point of view his sisters were always happy to oblige, but there was something about Mei that made him want to impress her. Something that made him want to be more than what he was. Who he was.

But finding out she had a kid changed all that.

He had decided long ago that he didn't

have the skills needed to be a parent. He didn't want to risk making the same mistakes he felt his own parents had made. And if he had no intention of being a father he definitely had no intention of being a stepfather, which meant it was easier not to start a relationship with a woman who already had a child. So, unless he was prepared to break his own rule, Mei was off-limits. There were plenty of women in the world. He didn't need to chase after one with a child.

'You look like you could use a drink.' His brother-in-law-to-be was by his side, holding out a beer. Jet hadn't had a drink all night, he had a big training session tomorrow, but one beer couldn't hurt. Maybe it would help him to sleep, help to keep his mind off Mei.

'Where's Mei?'

Jet sighed. Couldn't Ryder have picked a different subject? Anything else would have been good.

'She's gone home.'

'Already? What did you say to her?'

'Nothing.'

Well. Almost nothing. Maybe he should have said something. But what? Her announcement had taken him by surprise, but even with warning he wouldn't have changed his mind. He had a rule. He didn't date mothers.

Mei was exhausted. Because of Jet she'd experienced myriad emotions in the space of a couple of hours. Surprise, desire, disappointment, anger.

And now she was annoyed with herself. She wished she could dial down her physical reaction to Jet, she wished she could forget about him, but he was clearly at the forefront of her mind and almost the first thing she mentioned to her sister-in-law when she went to collect An Na in the morning.

'Did you have a good night?' Su-Lin asked.

Had she? She wasn't sure how to describe the evening exactly. 'It started off okay.'

'What happened?' Su-Lin switched on the coffee machine as she prepared to listen to Mei debrief.

Mei was happy to stay. An Na was not in a hurry to leave her cousins and Mei needed a sounding board. Su-Lin was always the voice of reason.

She sat at the kitchen bench and started talking. 'Jet was there.'

'With a partner? Is he dating a paramedic or married to one?'

'No. The party was for all the local first responders, I hadn't realised that. I was a little unprepared.'

'You talked to him?'

'Yes,' she said, although she neglected to mention she'd danced with him. That seemed irrelevant now. As did the fact that she was still attracted to him, that he made her feel things she hadn't felt in years. If she was going to be completely honest, which she wasn't, she hadn't felt like this about anyone else, not before and not after Jet. But it didn't matter how she felt when she was in his arms. He'd made it perfectly clear that he wasn't interested, and Su-Lin didn't need to hear all of that. It wasn't important now.

'Did you tell him?'

'I told him I had a child.'

'That was it?'

'It was hardly the right environment to

share the whole story and it was obvious he wasn't interested in me once he knew I was a single mother.' Mei checked behind her, making sure that none of Su-Lin's brood or An Na had come into the kitchen without being noticed. 'At least I don't need to worry about him wanting to take An Na away. He's not interested in being a father.'

'He said that?'

'He didn't need to.'

'He might change his mind if he knows he already has a child. You are still planning on telling him?'

Mei wasn't convinced. 'An Na and I are okay; maybe there's no need. We don't need to upset the apple cart.'

'Mei, it doesn't matter what you think. Jet needs to know. You need to think about An Na. What if she wants to find her father one day and then finds out you have kept them apart? You might not want Jet in your life but you can't make that decision for An Na. Or for Jet.'

'And what if he doesn't want anything to do with her? With us?'

'That's his call to make and it's one that

is better coming from him, not from you. You have to give him all the information and then see what choice he makes. You can't condemn him without giving him the facts. He needs the chance to make an informed decision.'

'What would you recommend?'

'You should tell him sooner rather than later, but if you do want to speak to a family lawyer first I can give you a couple of recommendations,' Su-Lin offered for the second time. 'It might be a good idea to get some information about custody situations.'

'I really don't think he's going to want custody,' Mei said. She could talk to a lawyer, but nothing would change the fact that Jet was An Na's father and if he wanted to be part of her life Mei knew she would let him. She would never deny her daughter that.

'What about child support then?'

'Child support? I'm not going to ask for child support. An Na is my responsibility.'

'The court won't see it that way.'

'I thought you said you weren't a family lawyer.'

'I have plenty of friends who have been through divorces.'

'I don't need a lawyer. Not yet,' she decided. 'I'll talk to him first. We're both adults. Hopefully he'll want what's best for An Na and we can work things out between us.'

She thought about how she'd felt last night in Jet's arms.

Maybe things would be okay. She just needed him to be honest with her.

Could she trust him to do that?

She thought so. She hoped so.

Jet was coming back to the lifeguard tower after a coffee run when he saw an ambulance driving down Campbell Parade. His heart started racing and he picked up his pace as he wondered if the ambulance was headed for the beach, wondered if Mei was in it.

He ducked across the promenade and reached the tower just as Ryder stepped out.

'What's going on?' he asked as the ambulance turned onto the promenade and headed in their direction.

'We've got an elderly lady with a suspected fractured hip.'

'Do you know who the ambos are?'

Ryder grinned. 'Not Mei, if that's what you're asking.'

He bit back his disappointment. He hadn't seen her since the Christmas party and he hadn't been able to stop thinking about her.

'Why don't you call past the station and ask her out?' Ryder suggested. 'You know you want to.'

'I told you, I don't date women with kids. That's too much responsibility. I prefer to keep things simple.'

'Maybe you should make an exception. She's clearly got under your skin; you've been grumpy ever since the Christmas party. It's your rule so there's no reason why you can't break it.'

Jet shook his head. 'No. I don't need to complicate my life. There are plenty of single women out there without kids,' he replied.

'Trust me, you don't want to live with regret. You should take the chance...that's assuming she's interested in you.' Ryder laughed and slapped him on the shoulder before going to meet the ambulance.

Jet returned to the tower, coffee in hand, and picked up a pair of binoculars to scan the beach. The beach was busy enough to keep him occupied while he tried not to think about Mei. There were plenty of other women in the world, in Bondi even.

That might be true, but he knew there weren't a lot of women out there who made him feel like Mei did.

But was she interested? He had no idea.

Was Ryder right? Should he test the water or would he be getting in over his head? Mei was different. Was that a good thing or a bad thing? Would he be asking for trouble?

He debated with himself for most of the morning, backwards and forwards, until finally he had enough. Until he finally realised there was only one option. He would put the ball in her court and see what she said.

He scribbled his number on a piece of paper and stuck it in the pocket of his shorts. If it was still there next time he saw her, if he hadn't gone into the ocean and destroyed the paper, he'd give her his number and leave it up to her to call him if she was interested. The decision would be Mei's.

He picked up the binoculars again and kept his eye on a group of teenage boys who were standing in a circle and kicking a soccer ball around. Ball games were banned on Bondi as the beach was often too crowded for ball sports to be played safely. He watched them for a few minutes, hoping they'd pack the ball away of their own accord, but when that didn't happen he decided he needed to go down to the sand and put a stop to their fun. He didn't enjoy spoiling someone's day but he'd seen too many accidents from wayward balls and knew it was better to be safe than sorry.

'I'm going down to speak to those boys,' he told Ryder when he returned to the tower.

He jogged through the soft sand towards them and, as he approached, one of the boys completely missed the ball and kicked another boy in the ankle. He collapsed in a heap and hadn't stood up by the time Jet reached them.

His ankle swelled immediately and he was unable to bear weight. Jet suspected the teenager had a fractured fibula and he called for the buggy and an ambulance. He crossed his fingers, hoping the ambulance would bring Mei.

By the time he got the boy into the buggy and back to the tower he could hear the siren of the approaching ambulance. The door opened and Mei appeared. Jet's heart leapt at the sight of her and he fought hard to keep the smile off his face.

'We're going to need the stretcher,' he told her as Alex started to assess the patient.

Mei nodded and turned on her heel to fetch it from the ambulance. Jet went with her but he knew she was wondering what he was doing.

'I don't need help,' she said as she opened the rear doors.

'I know. I have something for you.' He took the folded piece of paper from his pocket and handed it to her.

'What's this?'

'My phone number. I thought we might have a coffee some time.' He was surprised to find he was nervous.

She was frowning. 'I got the feeling you didn't date single mothers.'

Had he been that obvious or that easy to read?

'I don't,' he said. He didn't bother lying, there was no point; she could easily find out the truth from anyone who knew him. 'It's just a coffee,' he added, trying to downplay the invitation.

Mei nodded and tucked the paper into her chest pocket before pulling the stretcher from the ambulance and turning her attention to their patient. She gave him nothing and left him feeling that he might have just made a complete fool of himself.

'An Na, time to get ready for bed.'

An Na had been making dumplings, but she should have cleaned up her workstation ages ago. She was normally compliant about bedtime, but she was being resistant tonight and she was testing Mei's patience.

Mei was tired. She'd had a busy day at work and she was stressed over Jet. She had unfolded the piece of paper with his phone number on it so many times over the past few days that it was in danger of falling apart. She hadn't been able to bring herself to put his number into her phone but if she didn't do it soon the paper might disintegrate. Knowing she now could contact him, that he had unwittingly put the ball in her court, was making her fractious and she wasn't handling An Na's difficult behaviour well. Maybe she'd take over from her dad in the restaurant and he could put An Na to bed.

'An Na, do you want Ye Ye to read you a story?' she asked.

'If you're going out the front, can you take this order out?' her mum said as she handed her a takeaway order.

'Dad, do you want to take a break?' she asked as she put the carry bags on the counter. 'Would you mind reading An Na a bedtime story? She's resisting going upstairs but I think she'll listen to you. I'll look after things here for a bit.'

Mei was keen to get upstairs too, but she didn't have the energy to deal with An Na. It was one of the many difficult things about being a single mum. She thought again about how Jet had managed to escape all the hard years, the long hours. She realised he'd also missed out on all the joy, although some days, when she was so exhausted that her bones ached and she felt forty-six instead of twenty-six, it was harder to remember the good times.

She turned her head as the bell above the restaurant door jangled and Poppy walked in.

'Poppy, hello!'

'Mei! What are you doing here?'

'This is my parents' restaurant.'

'Your parents?'

Mei nodded. 'This is my dad—' she gestured a hand in her father's direction '—and Mum is the chef.'

'I had no idea!' Poppy declared. 'Ryder and I have eaten here so many times, the food is incredible. It's amazing that I've never seen you here.'

'I'm not regular wait staff, although I do help out around my ambo shifts,' Mei explained as An Na appeared from the kitchen.

'Hello, An Na,' Poppy greeted her.

'You know An Na?' Mei asked.

Poppy nodded. 'Of course, she's looked

after us often when we eat here. She brings our menus and our water.'

'Hello,' An Na acknowledged Poppy before asking Mei, 'Mum, is Ye Ye going to read to me?'

'An Na is your daughter?'

Mei nodded—she could hardly deny it but she felt a flutter of anxiety coupled with a spell of light-headedness. She held onto the counter for support as her worlds collided. How had she never seen Poppy and Ryder in the restaurant before? How could Poppy know An Na?

Poppy was Jet's sister. Jet hadn't asked An Na's age but what if Poppy said something? He could put two and two together as easily as the next person. There were too few degrees of separation now.

She really needed to speak to Jet. Preferably before Poppy did, but she couldn't ask her to keep An Na a secret without giving an explanation. Mei looked at the name on the takeaway order that her mum had given her; she hadn't paid attention to the name but it was obviously Poppy's.

'This is your order,' she said as she passed it over, hoping that would be enough to get her moving. Mei needed some time to think. 'Enjoy your dinner.'

Poppy left and Mei's father and An Na headed upstairs, leaving her alone at the counter. Why couldn't Poppy have come in ten minutes later, after An Na had gone upstairs? She knew it was only a matter of time now before Jet learned the truth. And she knew he needed to hear it from her.

'Has she called you yet?'

Jet and Ryder were sitting on the deck at Lily's house overlooking Bondi Beach and waiting for Poppy, who was picking up a takeaway on her way home from the ambulance station. All three of Jet's sisters—Lily, Poppy and Daisy—were living together and Jet, and Ryder, were frequent visitors.

'No.' He didn't know what to make of it. It had been a few days. He'd been sure Mei would call. But what if she didn't?

'So maybe your concerns about dating a single mother are unfounded. Looks like you might not get a chance.' Ryder laughed.

Of course, with Jet's competitive nature, the minute someone told him he couldn't do something he'd become desperate to prove them wrong. But he wasn't used to being in this situation. He wasn't used to waiting for a woman to be interested. He'd always been popular with women, had always been able to pick and choose, but now Mei had all the power and it was unsettling.

'Perhaps this is a good thing,' he said. 'I'd like to get to know her but it's not like I can just pretend her kid doesn't exist. It's probably better if she doesn't call. I don't like complicated women.'

'What makes you think she's complicated? There's a difference between a complicated woman and a complicated situation. I don't think you should give up on her yet.'

'Who are you talking about?' Poppy asked as she stepped out onto the deck and dumped the bags of takeaway on the table.

'Mei Chen,' Ryder said as he poured her a glass of wine.

'That's a coincidence,' Poppy said. 'I just saw her when I was picking up dinner. Her parents own Lao Lao's Kitchen. Why are you talking about her?'

'Your brother has given her his number but she seems to be resistant to his many charms and he's not sure what to do about it.'

'You're waiting for her to call you? Why don't you just ask her out?' Poppy said when he nodded.

'Because I have a rule—I don't date single mums. You know she has a kid?'

'I do.' Poppy nodded. 'She has a daughter and she's the cutest thing.'

'You've seen her?' Ryder asked as he unpacked the takeaway containers.

'Yes, you've met her too. It's An Na.'

'The waitress?'

'Waitress?' Jet was surprised. He hadn't asked her daughter's age but she couldn't be old enough to work. She must only be little. 'How old is she?'

Poppy laughed. 'Only young. She helps out in the restaurant, but waitress is a bit of a fancy term for a child. She's about seven.'

'Are you sure?'

'She's six or seven, around about that age. Why? Does her age make a difference?'

It didn't. At least, not in the way Poppy was thinking, but hearing that Mei's child— Mei's daughter—was that old made his head spin.

After Poppy's announcement it was impossible to focus. Dinner was a blur. He couldn't remember what he ate or the conversation. He hoped it mostly focused on Poppy and Ryder and their wedding plans. He hoped there wasn't anything he'd promised to do.

He kept doing the sums, over and over, in his head and as soon as they'd finished eating he excused himself.

His mind was racing as he walked down the hill towards home. Churning through multiple possibilities.

He'd been twenty when they'd met. Eight years ago. If Mei's daughter was six, he was off the hook. But what if she was seven? Who was the father?

Was he?

But surely Mei would have told him?

It mustn't be him. There was no real reason to think he had anything to do with it. Which meant it was either someone else... or was Mei not sure?

But he didn't think Mei was the type of girl who would have had multiple partners.

Which left the very real possibility that Mei's daughter could be much younger than seven. Poppy hadn't been certain of her age.

Or maybe Mei didn't want him to know?

His mind was still spinning when he reached the corner of his street. He needed an answer, one way or the other. He needed to know if he was a father. If he had a daughter.

Instead of turning for home, he continued walking. He was halfway to the Junction. Halfway to the Chinese restaurant that apparently Mei's parents owned. There was only one way to solve the puzzle. He'd go and see if the restaurant was still open. If Mei was there.

He'd find Mei now and confirm that her daughter wasn't his and then he'd get on with his life.

He was only a few metres from the restaurant when the outside lights were switched off, leaving just the sign over the awning illuminated.

He stopped at the door and peered through the glass. He could see a figure at the back of the restaurant. Was that Mei?

He rapped his knuckles on the door and waited as Mei crossed the room. She was peering through the darkness and her expression when she reached the door and saw it was him was not one of surprise. He noticed her hesitate before she unlocked the door and he had the feeling that if the door hadn't been glass, if he hadn't been able to see her, she would have left him standing on the footpath.

'You've seen Poppy,' she said as she opened the door. Her voice was flat, her words a statement, not a question.

He nodded. 'Your daughter,' he said as he wiped his clammy hands on his thighs. 'Is she mine?'

CHAPTER FIVE

'YOU'D BETTER COME IN.'

Mei stepped back and let him into the restaurant. The chairs had been upended on the tables in preparation for cleaning the floor and she lifted one chair off a table for two near the window and set it on its feet. Jet lifted the other and collapsed into it. His legs felt as if he'd run a half marathon and he knew if he didn't sit down he'd fall.

Mei sat opposite him. She hadn't turned on the restaurant lights but there was enough light coming through the window from the street to illuminate her face. She was biting her lip and looking anywhere but at him.

Jet's heart was racing and his hands trembled. He clenched them into fists to stop the shaking and said, 'She's mine, isn't she?'

Mei looked at him then, her eyes huge and dark, her face pale.

She nodded and Jet exhaled, letting go of a breath he hadn't been aware of holding. He felt nauseous, nervous, terrified. That wasn't how he wanted to feel but he couldn't control it.

Mei was watching him. She looked worried and he wondered if she was afraid of his reaction.

One of them had to speak, but what was the right thing to say? What was the appropriate response? He realised he'd convinced himself that Mei's child wasn't his. He'd expected her to say no. But that wasn't the case. With one nod Mei had upended his world and changed his life.

He had a child.

He was a father.

Was he prepared for that?

He knew he wasn't. Far from it.

He wasn't emotionally or mentally prepared. He had no idea how to be a parent. His own parents had hardly set a fine example and fatherhood was something Jet had been doing his best to avoid. This wasn't a situation he'd ever spent much time considering and he found himself floundering now.

He should have a thousand questions but his mind was blank. The idea that he had a child, a daughter, that he was a father, was quite incomprehensible. He needed some time to process the information.

'Her name is An Na.' Mei had obviously given up waiting for him to say something, which was fortunate as he couldn't think of a single sensible, suitable comment.

'An Na.' The unfamiliar sounds rolled around in his mouth. He had a daughter; she was real. A small piece of him existed in the world, separate and distinct from him, but a part of him all the same.

'It means quiet and graceful.'

'Is she?'

Mei smiled and her expression softened, changing in an instant from one of concern and caution to one of unconditional love. Jet recognised it and wondered if that was an emotion that was innate or learned. He suspected the former. Surely if love for your child could be learned his parents would have been more loving. But if it couldn't be learned he was in trouble.

'She can be.' Mei paused before adding, 'Just not very often.'

'And she's seven?'

Mei nodded. 'She turned seven in August.'

'Were you planning on telling me about her?'

'Of course.'

'When? When she was eight or eighteen?'

'I've been trying to work out when and how. I didn't want to spring it on you out of the blue after all this time.'

They sat in silence as Jet tried to sort through his emotions.

'What happens now?' Mei asked. He was glad she didn't try to justify her position any further.

'I have no idea. I need time to think. You had time.'

'No, I didn't,' she argued. 'One day I was a teenager, planning on going to medical school, and the next I was an eighteen-year-old girl who was pregnant and having to make choices about something I had never considered. But I get that this is a shock,

I get you'll need time, but please consider An Na in all of this. I know you said kids were not on your agenda, but none of this is her fault.'

'I know.'

He heard what she was saying but he couldn't make any promises. Not yet.

'Are you working tomorrow?' he asked.

'Night shift.'

'Can we meet for lunch?' He didn't know if his head would be any clearer by then, but he also knew he couldn't delay a serious conversation indefinitely. They would have a lot of things to talk about and work through.

'Shall I meet you here?' he asked when she nodded.

'No! Not here.'

'How about Tamarama Beach then?' Jet thought it would be good to be able to see the ocean; it would give clarity to his thoughts and Tamma was quieter than Bondi during the week.

'Can we go somewhere else?'

'Why? We'll get more privacy at the beach than we would in a restaurant.'

'I'm happy to avoid restaurants but I hate

eating at the beach; there is nothing worse than sand in your food.'

'Okay, let's meet at Bronte Park,' he suggested as a compromise. There was a picnic area on the headland that overlooked the ocean but avoided the sand and it was usually quiet on a weekday. 'I'll meet you at the surf club; I'll bring something to eat and we can have a picnic. That way, we won't have any interruptions.'

'Let me bring the food. My parents own a restaurant after all.'

Jet wasn't sure that he could face another meal of Chinese food. Tonight's dinner was sitting heavily in his stomach but he knew that wasn't a fault of the cooking or the food. It was purely and simply stress.

'No, it's okay, I've got this one.'

Jet walked the streets after leaving the restaurant as he tried to figure out what had just happened. He knew he was in shock, nothing life-threatening or critical but he was reeling from the news that he was a father. It was a surreal notion.

He knew it wouldn't feel real until he met her.

He should have asked to see a photograph of her. Mei must have had dozens on her phone. But he was so stunned he hadn't known what to say, what to think.

He wondered what his daughter looked like. Did she take after him at all? Had he passed on any traits?

What would she be like and what would she make of him?

Could he be the father she wanted or needed?

How would he know? He and his sisters had grown up in an unconventional family. He knew they'd had an unusual childhood and that their experience was vastly different to the majority of kids and that meant he had no real idea about what was normal.

And what did all this mean for him and Mei? He had never dated a single mother, but she was no longer just any single mother— she was the mother of his child. That didn't change the fact that he was still drawn to her, that she still set his pulse racing. But what did this news mean for them? What would their future look like?

He wasn't about to walk away from his responsibilities, but did those responsibilities extend to Mei?

What was the right answer? Was there one?

Mei checked the time on the clock in her car. She was running late to meet Jet and, to make matters worse, she couldn't find a parking space. She slowed to a crawl as she watched the pedestrians—hoping one of them would get into their car and create a space for her—as she tried to organise her thoughts before she saw Jet.

She'd tossed and turned all night, worried, stressed and anxious about today's discussion, but a quick catch-up with Su-Lin after dropping An Na at school had calmed her nerves a little. Mei had dissected every one of Jet's few words from last night's conversation, trying to guess where his head was at.

She had hoped he would be more enthusiastic but, once again, Su-Lin had been the voice of reason, pointing out that the news had been rather sprung on him.

Mei hoped he would embrace the idea of being a father because how would she explain the alternative to An Na? How could she tell her she'd found her father if he didn't want anything to do with her? With them?

A young girl up ahead had her keys in her hand and Mei pulled her car to the left, narrowly missing scraping her side mirror on a parked car as she waited to see where the girl went. She breathed a sigh of relief as the girl got into her car a few metres in front. Fortunately, the space was large enough for Mei to avoid needing to reverse park. It was never her forte and she knew in her current mindset it would be a risky manoeuvre. She parked without incident and was heading for the surf club when she heard Jet call her name. He was waiting by a picnic table and he looked relieved to see her. Was he not certain she'd turn up?

She had been tempted to postpone before realising there was no point in delaying the meeting. There was nothing to stop him from coming to the restaurant again and she was desperate enough at this stage to want to avoid that at all costs. She didn't want anyone to see him there and start asking questions, especially An Na.

'Hi. Thanks for coming.' He took one step towards her before stopping in his tracks and dropping his hands to his sides. She knew he'd been about to greet her with a kiss. It had been an instinctive move and one she would have been happy to receive but she saw the hesitation on his face. Saw the moment he second-guessed himself, the moment he wondered if he would be over-stepping boundaries.

How was it possible that she could inter-pret the thoughts and expressions of a man she barely knew and hadn't seen for eight years? Some thoughts, she told herself. She had no idea what he was thinking with re-gard to An Na. Maybe she was just project-ing her feelings, maybe they didn't have a real connection.

She would have been happy for him to kiss her, but it was probably wiser that he didn't. She knew it would cloud her thoughts and sway her judgement and she needed a clear head for the discussion that was to come. They had a lot to work out, not least what her news meant for them. Where it put them. But An Na had to be her priority.

'That's okay. Thanks for not making me go to the beach,' she said, extending an olive branch.

'I didn't realise you were so against the beach. I would never have guessed that about you, considering where we met.'

'I was only there because my friends were, but I don't hate the beach. I just really prefer to keep my food and sand separate and I'm not a strong swimmer.'

'So…' Jet smiled and her heart melted just a little. 'Apart from the sand and the sea, you have no objection to the beach.'

'None at all.' She laughed. 'An Na, on the other hand, loves the ocean. Any water. She'd spend her life swimming if she could.'

'Really?' He looked pleased and her heart softened a little more.

She nodded. 'She must get that from you. A definite case of nature over nurture.' She'd brought An Na into the conversation because, after all, that was why they were there, to discuss their daughter, not to exchange personal titbits about their lives as if they were on a first date. It wasn't a date.

She didn't want to feel the tingles, the connection. She needed to separate Jet, An Na's father, from Jet, the man who made her lose her train of thought, who made her heart race and her breath catch in her throat.

'I'm glad to know we will have something in common.'

'She has your smile too.'

'She does?'

Mei nodded. She took out her phone and showed him a photo. He still hadn't asked to see his daughter but she wasn't going to wait. The photo had been taken almost a year ago, but she'd chosen it deliberately—it was the one that most reminded her of Jet. The one that showcased An Na's smile—and the resemblance to Jet was unmistakable.

He looked at the photo in silence and this time she couldn't tell what he was thinking.

'I don't understand why you didn't tell me when you found out you were pregnant. I get that telling someone you don't know all that well they have a seven-year-old child isn't an easy thing to do and I appreciate you were intending to tell me, but why didn't you do that eight years ago?'

'I tried to. I came looking for you. I drove

up to Byron Bay with my sister-in-law. We went to your caravan but someone else was living there and they didn't know where you had gone. They didn't know you.'

'So that was it. You stopped looking?'

'I didn't know what else to do. We went to the beach, watched the surfers, but you weren't there. You'd told me you were going to travel. You were going surfing in Hawaii. How was I supposed to find you? I didn't even know your last name. For all I knew, you had already left town. If I had found you, what do you think you would have wanted? How would you have felt? Did you want to be a father at twenty-one?'

'No. Did you know right away you were going to keep the baby?' he asked.

'By the time I figured out I was pregnant it was too late to do anything else,' she answered honestly. 'I knew this was going to change my future, but An Na didn't deserve to pay the price for something I'd done. I chose to sleep with you, it was a conscious decision, and I chose to keep An Na. Getting pregnant was my mistake; it wasn't hers.'

'It was *our* mistake.'

Mei nodded. 'Maybe,' she agreed, 'but I don't think of it as a mistake any more.'

'Were you scared?'

'Terrified,' she admitted. 'But I think that's how every new parent feels.'

'So, it's not just me then?'

'No, it's not just you.'

'But you had time to grow with An Na. To learn, to make mistakes. If I make a mistake there's nowhere to hide. An Na will know. I don't want to let her down but I have no idea how to be a parent.'

'Do you have nieces and nephews?'

'No. I have three sisters but none of them have kids.'

'Your job is to love An Na, to guide her, to encourage her, to support her. To teach her that she can do anything, be anything. Teach her to be kind, help her to be happy.'

'But how do you do that? My sisters and I weren't taught any of that by our parents. My father loves two things—surfing and my mother. In that order. And my mother...' he sighed '...the best thing I can say about her is that she was distant. She had a difficult upbringing. She ran away from home, fell in love with my father. She sees him as her protector and sometimes I think he is *all* she sees. She isn't maternal at all. I don't think she ever really wanted kids and I certainly don't think she planned any of her pregnancies. Lily, Poppy and I were born within 22 months of each other. That's the very opposite of planned pregnancies. The only thing our father taught us was how to surf.'

'Who brought you up?'

'We grew up in a commune. Supposedly we were raised collectively, although I really think we raised ourselves. I moved off the commune and into my caravan the minute I turned eighteen. I got a job in a pub and spent my days surfing. I'm guessing your story is a bit different; most people are.'

'Our childhoods were probably chalk and cheese,' she admitted.

'Are you close to your parents?'

Mei smiled. 'I'm Asian, I don't really have a choice, but yes, I am. I still live with them. Things were rocky when I fell pregnant. That wasn't the life my parents had envisaged for me when they emigrated from Hong Kong when I was two. It wasn't the life I imagined either, but they have been supportive and An Na had has good male role models in my brother and my father. I'm not saying it's been easy, but we've got this far.'

'And now what? Where do we go from here?'

'I guess An Na and I need to know if you want to be a father now. It's a full-on commitment. What does your life look like now? Are you still surfing, travelling the world? That could make things complicated.'

'Surfing is just a hobby now. I enjoyed it but I wasn't having great success. I told myself I was too tall but the truth is I simply wasn't good enough. But while I was in Hawaii I competed in the Ironman series, a competition which started in Australia but I'd never been involved. Turns out my height and long limbs were an advantage in that sport, so I switched over.'

'Is that a professional sport too?'

'Semi-professional. I'm training and hoping to qualify for the World Championships next year. There is prize money for some events, and I have a couple of sponsorship deals, but I couldn't live off what I make. I need my job as a lifeguard.'

'So, you're still chasing your dream. I used to imagine you, travelling the world, chasing your dream. I resented you and your freedom after I gave my dream away.'

'Medicine?'

She nodded.

'Did you start the course?'

She shook her head. 'I knew it was going to be impossible to study medicine as a single mother. I wouldn't have the time or energy for years of intense study. I needed an income.' She shrugged. 'Paramedics seemed like a good compromise.'

'Has it been?'

'In a way, but I still have regrets. I still dream of being a doctor.'

'What's stopping you?'

She stared at him in disbelief. 'For the last seven years my purpose has been to raise An Na, to be a mother to An Na, to make sure I didn't fail her. I couldn't do both. Yes, I regret I didn't become a doctor, but I wouldn't change anything. I wouldn't give up being An Na's mother to be a doctor.'

'I'm not suggesting you have to give something up. I'm just asking what the barriers are.'

'I still need an income, for one thing, if I'm ever going to be able to move out of my parents' house and into one of my own, and even if I worked part-time a thousand other things are stopping me. Time, money, logistics.'

'We can work something out financially. An Na is my responsibility too now.'

'We don't need your money.' That wasn't true but her pride wouldn't let her admit it. Besides, it didn't sound as if he had much money to spare.

'Maybe not, but it is my responsibility. I want to help.'

'What we need to do is to work out a plan going forwards. I need to know how involved you want to be. Are you going to be a part of An Na's life or just send a cheque in the mail once a month?'

'You know no one sends cheques any more, right?' Jet was smiling.

'This isn't funny.'

'Mei,' he said. He reached across the table

and held her hand and her stomach somer-saulted in her belly. 'I spent most of the night thinking about this and I have to admit that I haven't come close to getting my head around the situation. I have no idea how to be a father. It wasn't something I ever thought I'd be, but I don't walk away from my re-sponsibilities. I am a grown-up, an adult. I'm not twenty any more. My concern is that I might not be able to be a good father and will that do An Na more harm than good? I need some time to process this but I would like to meet her.'

Mei nodded. She knew it was a reasonable and logical request, but she wanted him to think about what that meant before he met his daughter.

'Once you meet her you are committed to being her father. Walking away then would be more damaging to her than not knowing I'd found you in the first place. If I intro-duce you, do you understand you're making a commitment, a promise to her?'

'I do.'

Mei took a breath. 'Okay, give me a few

days to break the news to her. Why don't we meet for breakfast on Sunday? You can meet her then.'

CHAPTER SIX

JET WATCHED THE beach from his post in the North Bondi tower. The morning sun had finally risen high enough so it was no longer shining directly into his eyes and he removed his sunglasses and picked up the binoculars as he scanned the water. The conditions weren't favouring the surfers but there were plenty of swimmers making the most of a warm Saturday and the beach was busy. The north end was popular with families and also with the teenagers who were constantly coming off second best when launching themselves into the ocean from Flat Rock.

Jet was working with a rookie lifeguard who was full of questions. Usually he would be impressed with his enthusiasm but, this morning, he just wanted peace and quiet. He needed time to think. Tomorrow he would be meeting his daughter for the first time and he was on edge.

What if she didn't like him? What if he didn't know what to say? He'd had limited experience with kids and he'd been wondering if he should seek advice from his sisters, but what could they tell him that he couldn't figure out for himself?

Lily was the one he usually turned to for advice but he was worried about discussing An Na with her, given her situation. Lily's marriage had broken down after she'd suffered a miscarriage and Jet knew she still hadn't completely recovered. He didn't want the news about An Na to open old wounds. He could talk to Daisy, she was a paediatric nurse and was brilliant with kids, but she would also have myriad questions for him and he doubted he would have the answers.

He needed some more time to figure things out before he divulged his news. He needed a chance to make arrangements with Mei before his sisters chimed in with their ideas. He knew they would mean well but they wouldn't be able to help themselves and he wasn't sure their input would be taken in context by Mei. She might consider it interfering and, after raising An Na for seven years on her own, he knew she had a right to her opinion. Besides, what guidance could his siblings really offer? They might know how to talk to kids, but they certainly couldn't offer any parenting advice. None of the Carlson siblings had any idea of what normal parenting looked like. Their upbringing had been unconventional to say the least.

He also knew that the moment he told his sisters about An Na they would want to meet her and he didn't want to swamp Mei or An Na with his family. He needed time to establish a relationship with his daughter first.

And what about his relationship with Mei? What would that look like going forward? He was having difficulty separating the idea of her as a mother, his daughter's mother, and someone he felt emotionally and physically drawn to.

He needed to prioritise the issues, he had to consider one thing at a time and the first thing needed to be An Na. His first priority was working out how to be a father. He didn't think he could handle starting a relationship with Mei at the same time. That was too much pressure. He had no experience in either of these areas and it was highly likely that he would be biting off more than he could chew if he pursued a relationship with Mei while he was trying to figure out parenthood. He didn't want to fail. His focus had to be An Na, which meant that everything else would have to wait.

He needed some thinking time but it was difficult when he was being peppered with questions by the rookie lifeguard. He was about to suggest to the rookie that he go for a walk to patrol the water's edge when a radio call came through from the main tower.

'North Bondi, this is Central.'

'Go ahead, Central.'

'We've got reports of bluebottles at the south end. They'll be heading your way. You might want to alert the swimmers.'

'Roger that.'

The bluebottles, officially known as Portuguese man-of-war, were jellyfish whose long tentacles could wrap themselves round swimmers and inflict painful stings. While they were venomous, the most common symptom amongst the beachgoers was intense pain.

Jet had seen many people suffering extreme pain and those under the age of thirty seemed less able to stand the discomfort. The beach had plenty of people in that age group today. Rather than wait for the inevitable as treating bluebottle stings had a tendency to stretch the lifeguards' resources, Jet would do his best to warn the swimmers and clear the water.

The red and yellow flags were flapping in the breeze, indicating the change in the wind direction. He knew the little sails on the tops of the jellyfish would be catching the wind and it was only a matter of minutes before the troublesome sea creatures would arrive at his end of the beach.

'Lewis, the southerly is blowing bluebottles into shore—we need to clear the water,' he instructed the rookie lifeguard. 'I'll head down to the water to let the swimmers know. Can you erect some warning signs?' Yellow warning signs were stacked underneath the tower, but Lewis would need to dig some holes in the sand to hold them. That was a job for a junior, Jet thought as he grabbed the megaphone and backpack and leapt down from the tower.

Before he reached the water's edge he could see several people already emerging and complaining of stings.

'Don't pull the tentacles off with your fingers,' he warned a pair of teenage boys. 'It'll just transfer the venom to your hands as well.' He pulled a disposable glove from his backpack and handed it to them. 'Use this and then head up to the pavilion; a hot shower is the best remedy.' The quicker they got under the shower, the sooner their symptoms would ease and usually within a half hour of being stung people had recovered. They might be left with angry welts on their skin but the pain normally settled relatively fast.

As he finished with the teenagers a man standing in the shallows called out and waved Jet over. 'I need help, please. My niece has been stung—she's having trouble breathing.'

There were three young children, two girls and a boy, with the man and Jet could see red welts on their skin. Two of the children were yelling in pain but one young girl was quiet and Jet was immediately on high alert. The volume of a child's reaction to an injury was usually a good indicator of the level of pain and the quieter a child was, the more the lifeguards worried.

Allergic reactions to bluebottle stings were rare but Jet knew they could occur. The man had picked the girl up and she was clinging to his side while the boy continued to wail. Jet could see an angry red welt on the girl's throat. Stings on the limbs or trunk were painful enough; he could only imagine how one on the tender flesh of a throat would feel and if it was associated with swelling it was a dangerous situation.

'Is she allergic to anything else? Bees?'

'I don't think she's ever had a bee sting.'

The girl's eyes were wide with fear and she was going pale. She was still breathing but Jet knew time was critical. He needed to get her to the tower. Quickly. He needed two buggies and an ambulance.

He called the tower requesting backup and then spoke to the girl's uncle.

'Give her to me and I'll meet you at the

tower,' he told him. 'I need to get her there quickly. Other lifeguards are on the way and they'll help you with the other children.'

He took the little girl. She was light but limp in his arms and he was breathing heavily as he jogged through the sand, heading for the tower and keeping an eye out for the buggy.

'You're going to be okay,' Jet told her as Ryder pulled up in the ATV. Jet jumped into the passenger seat, cradling the girl on his lap. 'Go, go,' he said to Ryder. His priority was to get her to the tower to treat her there. He just prayed the ambulance would hurry.

Ryder parked the buggy at the steps to the tower and Jet was out of the vehicle before Ryder had killed the engine. He ran up the stairs and laid his patient on the treatment plinth. She was as limp as a rag doll and barely breathing.

Gibbo was waiting for them. 'The ambos are a couple of minutes away, but they've said to administer the EpiPen if her condition is still deteriorating.'

The girl's eyes were closed and Jet knew she wasn't aware of her surroundings.

'I think we have to,' he said. Her condition was critical and they couldn't afford to wait another minute, let alone two.

Gibbo handed him the adrenalin pen. Jet removed the blue lid and pressed the orange end against the girl's thigh, pushing hard until he heard it click. He counted to three and held it a fraction longer, just to be sure the adrenalin had been administered, before lifting it off her leg. He looked at the clock on the wall above the desk and noted the time, hoping he wouldn't need to give a second dose and knowing he'd need to tell the paramedics the time he'd injected the first.

He slipped an oxygen mask over her face as an extra precaution and stood beside the treatment plinth and watched, willing the drug to work as he waited for the girl's breathing to ease.

He could hear the ambulance siren now, its volume increasing as it approached, and he felt the tension dissipate from his body as his shoulders relaxed.

There were still some tentacles clinging to the girl's arm and leg and he pulled on a pair of surgical gloves and began to gently remove them while Gibbo sponged the welt on her neck with hot water, trying to take some of the sting out of the venom.

The ambulance siren cut out as Jet lifted the last tentacle from the girl's thigh. Her breathing had improved but she wasn't out of the woods yet and he was eager to hand her care over to the paramedics.

The door to the tower opened and he immediately looked over, hoping to see Mei. He knew she was working today, but it was the girl's uncle who entered. Jet took one look at him and could see he was still in a state of panic.

'She's okay,' Jet reassured him. 'She's breathing more easily and the ambos have arrived.'

The girl's uncle turned to face the door as it opened again, this time admitting Poppy and Mei. Mei led the way and he tried to catch her eye over the heads of the others but, before she could look in his direction, the girl's uncle had intercepted her.

'Mei!'

'Bo? What are you doing here?'

Jet listened in slight confusion, trying to

work out the relationship between them as the uncle explained the situation. 'Mei, it's An Na—she's been stung.'

'An Na?'

Jet turned back to the plinth. An Na? This little girl was An Na? His daughter?

'An Na.' Mei pushed past the lifeguards, forcing her way through the congested space until she reached the plinth.

She was standing next to him, but Jet knew she hadn't seen him as she slid her arms under her daughter and held her.

His first instinct was to do the same for Mei. To hold her, to protect her, to comfort her and reassure her, but she wasn't even aware of his presence. She was completely oblivious to everything around her, intent only on her daughter. She hugged her and then laid her flat again. She brushed An Na's hair from the side of her face with one hand, tucking it behind the strap of the oxygen mask and held An Na's wrist with the other, feeling for her pulse as she watched the rise and fall of her chest. An Na's breathing was still laboured and her skin was crisscrossed with angry welts.

'What happened?' Mei was speaking to him now, but he still wasn't sure if she was taking things in. She would have been told the details of the incident when she'd received the emergency call, but it was clear her mind had gone blank. Her eyes were glazed and he suspected she just saw a random lifeguard. He certainly didn't think she'd registered that it was him she was speaking to.

'She had an anaphylactic reaction to a jellyfish. She's been given one dose of adrenalin.' He tried to set her mind at ease, but he doubted she was really listening. It was impossible to expect her to be impartial, to respond as a paramedic when the patient was her own daughter. He needed to let Poppy know what had transpired.

He turned around, desperately seeking his sister.

'This is Mei's daughter,' Poppy explained. She was talking to him as if this was just any patient and he was momentarily confused, but of course, from Poppy's point of view An Na was just an ordinary patient.

'How long ago did you administer the adrenalin?' Poppy asked as she wrapped a blood pressure cuff around An Na's arm and clipped an oximeter to her fingertip.

Jet checked the clock. 'Ten minutes.' He frowned. Had it really only been ten minutes? It felt like a lifetime.

'And her breathing's improved?' Poppy confirmed.

Jet nodded.

'Mei? Does An Na have any other allergies?' Poppy spoke quietly to her colleague, gathering information but not expecting any contribution in terms of treatment from her.

Mei shook her head as Jet stood there, not sure what was needed of him, not sure if he was needed at all, but he couldn't bring himself to step away. He remained in place, as a spectator. There was no role for him. An Na didn't know him and, with the exception of Mei, no one knew he was An Na's father.

'Okay, she's stable,' Poppy said as Jet let himself relax just slightly, 'but she needs to go to hospital for observation.'

Jet knew there was a danger of a second allergic reaction once the adrenalin from the EpiPen wore off. 'Are you ready to move her now?' he asked Poppy. The ambulance stretcher didn't fit inside the tower and it was always easier to carry the light patients out rather than transfer them to a chair or spinal board, but he wasn't going to give anyone else the opportunity to carry An Na. She was his daughter and the incident today had terrified him. He could have lost her before he'd even met her.

Poppy nodded, giving Jet the all-clear, and he touched Mei's shoulder. 'Mei, let me carry her.'

Mei finally registered his presence. She nodded and stepped back as he scooped An Na up off the plinth.

Her head rested on his chest and he hugged her to him. She'd opened her eyes briefly when Mei had spoken to her, but her eyelids had fluttered closed again. Her eyelashes were thick and dark against the pale skin of her cheeks and this time Jet concentrated on how it felt to hold his child in his arms.

He wanted to feel a connection. He'd imagined there would be some sense of recognition when he first met his daughter, although he hadn't imagined it would be under these circumstances, and it disap-

pointed him to know that he'd had no in-
kling, that there had been no sense that she
was part of him. She was delicate and warm,
but she felt like any other child in his arms.

He badly wanted to feel a connection and
now he just had to hope it would develop, but
he was terrified that it wouldn't. Perhaps he
would turn out to be like his parents.

Poppy opened the rear doors of the ambulance and pulled the stretcher out but didn't
disengage it from its rails. Jet laid An Na on
the sheet and Poppy strapped her in securely.

'Are you going to be okay in the back with
her?' Poppy asked Mei, obviously thinking
she was in no fit state to drive. 'I can call for
backup if you like.'

'No, I'm okay.'

Poppy pushed the stretcher into the ambulance and made certain it locked in place.
Mei climbed in and Poppy closed the doors
and Jet lost sight of his daughter.

As the ambulance departed he knew he
couldn't just let them go like that. Not An
Na or Mei.

Dutchy was off-duty but at the beach and
Jet convinced him to take over his shift.

'I need to go,' he told Dutchy and Gibbo. 'There's something I have to do.' He stalled any questions by adding, 'I'll explain later.'

Poppy was loading the empty stretcher back into the ambulance when Jet arrived at the hospital. He waited until she turned away from him before he ducked through the emergency entrance. He didn't want to answer questions about what he was doing there—he wasn't completely sure himself—but he couldn't stay at the tower; he had to get to the hospital.

He'd been consumed with fear at the idea that he could have lost An Na and his fear was tinged with anger at Mei for keeping her secret, even though he knew he was being unfair.

He'd managed to avoid Poppy on his way into the emergency department, but he hadn't counted on running into Lily.

'Jet! What are you doing here?'

Bumping into Lily was probably a good thing. He wouldn't be able to see An Na; he had no rights. He was her father but only as a technicality, not legally. Not yet.

'The patient Poppy brought in…a little girl? Do you know if she's okay?'

'You know I can't discuss my patients with you.'

'So, she is your patient?' All he needed now was for An Na to be admitted onto the paediatric ward and for Daisy to be the nurse, but he couldn't subject An Na or Mei to all his sisters in one go. Not here. Not today. His life was complicated enough, but somehow he had to find out how An Na was. 'Is Mei with her?'

'What's going on?'

Jet ignored her question. He really didn't have time to explain. 'Can you tell Mei I'm here? I need to speak to her.'

'I don't think she'll want to leave An Na to come out and talk to you,' Lily said. 'What is this about?'

'I'll explain later. Please, just pass on the message.'

Lily frowned but agreed. She left him pacing backwards and forwards in the emergency department as she went to deliver his message.

Jet imagined this was how expectant fathers would have felt back in the day, waiting for news. Things had changed now though— if Mei had told him about her pregnancy he would have been in the delivery room, not pacing the corridors and wearing out the linoleum floor. But would his twenty-one-year-old self have wanted anything to do with a baby? The truth was he wouldn't have been ready then. He'd still been growing up himself. He'd been self-absorbed, focused on his dreams, his goals—would he have wanted to derail those? He knew the answer was no, but what about now? Was he ready now?

He still hadn't achieved his goal of qualifying for the World Championships. It was so close he could almost touch it, but what if he had to give it up for An Na? Was he prepared to?

He didn't know the answer and he wasn't about to abandon An Na and Mei, at least he didn't think he was, but he was considering turning around and walking out of the door to give himself time to think when Mei appeared.

'The doctor told me you wanted to speak

to me,' she said. 'She's another one of your sisters?'

Jet nodded.

'She didn't seem to know why you needed to see me.' She paused while Jet shook his head. 'You haven't told your sisters about An Na?'

'No. I wanted to meet An Na first. To get to know her and for her to get to know me before I introduced you both to my sisters. Is An Na okay?'

'She will be.'

'Can I see her?'

Mei nodded and Jet followed her into the treatment bay.

An Na was sleeping.

'I can't believe she's mine,' he said as he studied her face, searching for any similarity, anything to connect her to him, but all he could see was a little girl, covered in red welts, who looked just like her mother.

'She looks like you when she is smiling. She walks like you too, light on her feet and bouncy, and she has your long fingers.'

'How did you know what I was thinking?'

Mei shrugged. 'It makes sense that you

would be looking for traces of yourself in her, but I often feel like I know what you're thinking.'

'Are you able to stay with her? What about your shift?'

'Alex is coming to relieve me. Poppy is waiting out the front in case we get called out on a job before Alex can get here and my sister-in-law is on her way. She'll stay with An Na if I can't.'

'And tomorrow?' They were supposed to be meeting for pancakes in the morning.

'An Na should be fine. I'll message you later to let you know and I'll confirm in the morning. Okay?'

Jet was reluctant to leave but he knew he couldn't stay. There was only supposed to be one relative with An Na at a time. He left Mei with An Na and returned to the waiting area, where he ran into Lily again.

She looked enquiringly at him. 'What's going on?'

'An Na is my daughter.'

'Your *what*?'

'My daughter.'

Lily's mouth fell open but before she could

ask any more questions her pager went off. Jet thought for a moment she was about to ignore it, before common sense prevailed.

He knew she would have to go but he also knew there would be explanations needed and it would be easier for him if he only had to tell his story once.

'Can we get together tonight?' he asked. 'All of us? Poppy and Daisy too. I'll explain everything then.'

CHAPTER SEVEN

JET'S SISTERS' QUESTIONS were flowing thick
and fast after his announcement about An
Na but he didn't have the answers for many
of them.

'How long have you known?'

'Only a few days. I knew Mei had a child,
but I assumed it was little...two or three at
the most,' he said to Poppy. 'When you said
you'd met Mei's daughter, and told me how
old she was, it made me wonder and I went
to see Mei. That was when she told me.'

'When did you meet Mei?' Daisy asked.

'Obviously about eight years ago,' Poppy
said.

Daisy glared at her while Jet replied, 'She
came to Byron Bay for a holiday when she
finished school. I met her then.'

'Why didn't Mei tell you about An Na years ago?'

'She says she tried to find me but by the time she realised she was pregnant I'd left the country. Gone to Hawaii.'

'I can't believe you're a dad. And we are all aunties! What are you going to do now?'

'I don't know. We haven't had time to figure it out. I hadn't met An Na until today. Mei was going to bring her to meet me tomorrow.'

'How are you feeling?'

'Overwhelmed. Worried. Nervous. I have no idea how to be a father and Mei doesn't seem overly confident in me either.'

'What did she say?'

'She said she thought I wouldn't want the responsibility or commitment of being a father. She didn't think I was someone she could rely on and that she and An Na would be better off with her family.'

'She said that now?'

'No. That was when she found out she was pregnant, but what if she still thinks that?'

'You're not born knowing how to be a parent. You'll learn as you go.'

'But it's different learning with a baby. An Na is seven; she'll know if I muck things up and so will Mei. She's had years to get it right. What if I fail? It's not like we've had great role models.'

'Your responsibility is to teach her how to be a good person. How to be kind. To love her. You can do that,' Lily told him, echoing Mei's sentiments.

'I feel like if it was going to be a natural or instinctive thing I would have felt a connection today on the beach. When I was holding An Na, I should have had some sort of sixth sense.'

'I think you're being a little harsh on yourself.'

'And what about Mei?' Poppy asked. 'I know you like her—does this change anything?'

'I don't know. Probably. My priority is getting to know An Na. I can't think about Mei right now.'

Mei and An Na were already at the North Bondi RSL Club when Jet arrived the next morning. As he approached their table he heard Mei tell An Na to go and ask for some colouring pencils. The tables were covered with white paper for kids to draw on but he did wonder why she sent An Na off as soon as he arrived.

'I haven't had time to tell her about you yet,' she explained when he asked the question. 'I was going to tell her last night but the trip to hospital put paid to that. Is it okay if we don't say anything this morning? You can just get to know her a little?'

He nodded in agreement, knowing there was no time for discussion.

'An Na, this is Jet,' Mei introduced him when An Na returned to the table clutching a cup filled with pencils. 'He's one of the lifeguards who helped you yesterday when you got stung by the jellyfish. Do you remember him?'

'No.'

'Hello, An Na. You tangled with a pretty nasty jellyfish yesterday—how are you feeling today?' He was a little hesitant to ask as he didn't want to raise any fears she might now have. He wasn't used to second-guessing himself and he wanted to make a good impression on Mei and An Na.

'I'm okay. A bit itchy. Do you want to see the marks?'

'Sure.'

An Na pushed the sleeve of her T-shirt up to show him the welts on her arm. They had faded but were still obvious. 'I had to go to hospital.'

'I know.'

'Are you going to have breakfast with us? We're having pancakes.'

An Na chatted away almost non-stop throughout breakfast. She was more than happy to have a captive audience and all that was required of Jet was to make a few interested remarks occasionally. She told him about her cousins and school. She told him about her favourite movie and her favourite subjects.

'And when you're not at school—what do you do then?'

'I go to ballet and tap classes and I'm learning the violin.'

'That sounds busy. Do you like that?'

'It's okay, but I really want to have surfing lessons. Do you know how to surf?'

'I do, actually.'

'Can you teach me?'

'If it's okay with your mum.' He knew he wasn't playing fair, but he didn't think Mei would refuse and he was happy to offer. It would give him a chance to spend some time getting to know An Na. His daughter.

He had no doubt that there were plenty of other skills she would need that he was not equipped to teach her, but this was something he could do and he was pleased to know the bluebottle incident hadn't put An Na off the beach.

'I guess so.' Mei nodded.

'Can we go surfing now?'

'No,' Mei replied. 'We have some things to do today. We'll sort out a time later.'

'Promise?'

'I promise.'

Jet paid for breakfast and walked with Mei to her car while An Na skipped ahead.

'She's amazing,' he said, 'but I'm wondering if you chose the right name for her. She's anything but quiet. It won't take long before I feel like I know her.'

Mei smiled. 'I think I just imagined that she'd take after me a bit more. I was quiet.'

It was blowing his mind that this little girl was part of him. He wanted her to know who he was. He stopped in his tracks and turned to Mei. 'I want to tell her who I am.'

'Now?'

'Yes. You know we'll be telling her at some point and if I'm going to take her surfing this week I think it's the right thing to do.'

'You're going to start this week?'

'I can pick her up from school.'

An Na turned back and tugged on Mei's hand as they walked down Campbell Parade.

'Can I have an ice cream?'

'You just finished breakfast!'

'I'm still hungry.'

'I reckon I could fit an ice cream in too,' Jet said. 'Why don't I buy us both one? You can have one as well, if you like, Mei, and then we can sit on that bench over there and eat them. What's your favourite flavour, An Na?'

'Chocolate.'

'Mine too.'

Jet caught Mei's eye as he paid for the ice creams and raised an eyebrow. She gave a slight nod but said nothing until they had their ice creams and were sitting on a bench looking over the sea.

'An Na, we have something to tell you.'

An Na looked at her mother and then at Jet. 'Are you Mummy's boyfriend? Isabella's mummy has a boyfriend.'

'No, that's not it. You know how I told you your daddy lives overseas?'

An Na nodded. 'In Hawaii.'

'Yes, that's right. Except he doesn't live there any more. Now he lives here, in Sydney.'

'He's here?'

'He's right here. Jet isn't my boyfriend, he's your dad.'

An Na turned to look at Jet. Ice cream dribbled down her arm, but she didn't seem perturbed by that or by Mei's announcement. 'Did you come to see me?' she asked.

'Yes,' Jet told her. It seemed like the best answer.

'Are you going to live with us?'

'No, I have my own house.'

'Are we going to live with you?'

He should have anticipated there would be plenty of questions, but he didn't know the answer to this one. He looked to Mei.

'No. Lao Lao and Ye Ye would miss us.'

'They could come too.'

'They need to stay at the restaurant.'

'Do you have other children? Do I have a brother or a sister?'

'No.' Jet finished his ice cream and licked his fingers. 'Why don't I take you for your first surfing lesson after school one day this week and you can ask me as many questions as you like then?'

'Okay.' An Na slipped her hand into his as they walked around the corner to Mei's car. Her little hand was soft and somewhat sticky, but with that gesture Jet knew what it felt like to be a father. He knew he would do whatever it took to make An Na proud of him.

'Thank you,' Jet said to Mei as An Na climbed into the car.

'What for?'

'You obviously haven't dragged my name

through the mud as far as An Na is concerned. She doesn't seem to hold any ill will
towards me.'

'I had no reason to try to set her against
you. You did nothing wrong by her,' Mei said
as she slid behind the wheel.

As she drove away he wondered about
what Mei hadn't said.

Did she feel he'd done wrong by her?

'Mummy, Mummy, did you see me? I was
surfing!'

An Na ran up the beach to where Mei was
sitting on a towel. She was bursting with
excitement and Mei hugged her daughter
tightly and said, 'That looked like so much
fun.'

Over the top of An Na's head Mei could
see Jet coming towards them, his surfboard
tucked under one arm, and from behind the
safety of her sunglasses she admired his long
lean frame, taut abdominals and broad shoulders. She wasn't a fan of the ocean but she
could see that there were certainly some ben-
efits to spending time at the beach.

'Can I go back in the water?' An Na asked as Jet lowered his board to the sand.

'Don't go in too deep,' Mei cautioned as An Na skipped back to the waves.

'And stay between the flags,' Jet added.

'She absolutely loved that, thank you. I wish you could have seen the expression on her face when you stood her up on the board.' Jet had been standing behind An Na; he'd lifted her onto her feet as they'd surfed in on a wave, not once but several times. The delight and sheer joy on An Na's face had made Mei's heart sing. 'Actually, you might be able to. I took a video. It might be clear enough.' She picked up her phone and opened the video as Jet sat on the sand beside her.

He didn't bother drying off and the water droplets on his skin glistened in the late afternoon light. He smelt of the ocean and she could feel the coolness of the water radiating from his body in contrast to the warmth of the day. She resisted the urge to lean in against him. But it wasn't easy. Whenever he was near she could feel herself being drawn to him and it took all of her willpower to control her impulses.

She passed him her phone and prepared herself for the rush of heat she knew she would experience when their fingers touched.

He hit 'play' and she waited while he watched the video. 'She's got good balance,' he said as the video finished. 'She'll be surfing in no time. Imagine what she'd be like now if she'd started surfing a few years ago.'

'If our paths had crossed earlier, you mean?'

'I'm not having a go, but I keep thinking about all the years I've missed. If you didn't have such an aversion to the beach we might have crossed paths again sooner,' he said as he smiled and returned her phone to her.

'It's not the beach I dislike, it's the ocean. I got washed off a sand bank and caught in a rip when I was about An Na's age. It absolutely scared the life out of me and ever since I've been wary of the water.'

'I can take you in. You'd be safe with me.'

Mei could almost imagine how it would feel to be in the water with Jet. To have his arms around her as if they were dancing. She wouldn't be afraid of drowning while he held her in his arms, but she would be afraid of other things.

'I'm okay here, thanks. If you can teach An Na to surf that's enough for me.'

'Well, let me know if you change your mind.'

'I will.'

Mei closed her eyes for moment as she let her mind wander. What was the future going to look like for her and Jet? Did she dare ask?

Was there a possibility that they could have a relationship? Not as An Na's parents but as a couple? Would there be a chance to explore that, or had that opportunity passed them by?

She couldn't ignore the fact that she was still attracted to him, but how did he feel about her?

Mei arrived home from work and headed for the restaurant kitchen, eager to find out how An Na's second surfing lesson went today.

'Where's An Na?' she asked, expecting to find her making dumplings or doing home-work at the bench, but she wasn't anywhere to be seen.

'In the restaurant. She's having dinner with her father.'

'With her father?' Mei swallowed nervously. Jet was here? Her hands were suddenly sweaty and she wiped them on her trousers before going into the restaurant.

Jet and An Na were sitting at a table sharing a bowl of dumplings and Mei's stomach rumbled as she sat down with them.

'Mummy! Guess what? I surfed all by myself today!'

'You did! That's fantastic. Well done!' Mei congratulated her daughter with a kiss on her forehead before turning to Jet. 'What are you doing here? I thought Bo was bringing An Na home?'

'An Na wanted to show me what she made at school today.'

'Oh?' She turned to her daughter. 'What did you make?'

'We decorated our tops for the Christmas concert. And Daddy said he'd come to watch me.'

'You did?'

Jet nodded. 'I did. So, I had a good day. I got invited out and I got to meet your parents. I wasn't sure when you were planning on introducing me.'

She wasn't sure either. She'd been nervous about that meeting but was kind of relieved now that he had taken it out of her hands.

'You can relax. I think your parents like me,' he said.

Did he know she'd been worried about that? She had been reluctant to introduce them, nervous about how it would go and what her parents might say. Although they understood that Jet hadn't known about An Na, she knew they would now expect him to take responsibility. She was sure he'd charmed her parents, but did he understand their expectations? Would he be prepared to step up?

She needed to know what his plans were—she needed some time alone with him to suss out his thoughts. Mei picked up the empty dumpling bowl and passed it to An Na.

'An Na, can you go and ask Lao Lao for some more dumplings, please?'

'Out with it,' Jet said as soon as An Na had disappeared into the kitchen.

'What?'

'There's obviously something on your mind. You sent An Na off so you could ask me something in private. What do you want to know?'

'You've taken An Na surfing twice and met my parents. You've obviously got an idea of the direction this is heading with An Na and I'm just wondering if we're going to have a chance to sit down together and have a conversation about what we're doing.'

'Are you asking what my intentions are?'

'Maybe.'

'To be honest, I haven't figured that out yet. I think getting to know An Na needs to be my priority. I don't know if I can do more than that at this stage. But if you want to organise a time to talk you can. I gave you my number—you *can* call me.'

'Oh.' Was she going to have to make the first move? She wasn't sure if she was brave enough for that.

'Mei, it's okay.' Jet reached out and placed his hand over hers and squeezed her fingers as An Na returned with more dumplings. 'Gibbo and his wife are hosting a barbecue for the lifeguards in a couple of days. It's a

Christmas tradition—he does a turkey, we sing carols, everyone dresses up. Come with me, have some fun and I promise we will find time to work out a plan going forwards.'

'That dress suits you,' Jet said as he opened the car door for her and took her hand to help her out.

'Thank you. An Na and Su-Lin picked it out for me.'

Mei was wearing one of only a few dresses she owned, a black silk dress with spaghetti straps and a flowing skirt. Su-Lin had chosen it for her and had helped her with her make-up. She'd applied red lipstick and a thick coat of mascara with just a touch of powder to highlight her cheekbones. Her hair was pulled back off her face. Su-Lin had gone for the casual, effortless, 'I'm not wearing any make-up' make-up.

'An Na didn't mind that you were going out without her?'

'No, she loves staying with her cousins overnight; she'd happily do it every night. But she did want me to invite you to do something with us tomorrow. She told me you had the afternoon free.' Mei wondered when Jet might think to share his schedule with her rather than her having to hear it from An Na.

'I'm doing a half day, starting at six, finished by one. Does that fit in with your plans? What are you doing?'

'Going to the mall to see Father Christmas. We can go in the afternoon if you'd like to come.'

She could see a moment of hesitation on his face. 'Are you busy?'

'No, I'll work around it. I don't want An Na to feel that I don't have time for her. I know what that's like and I don't want that for her. I'll be there.'

'Thank you.'

Mei took a deep breath as they opened Gibbo's front gate. She was nervous. This was the first social occasion she had been to with the lifeguards since they'd found out about Jet's history with her...since they'd found out about Jet's daughter...but she needn't have worried. Everyone was lovely and welcoming and she soon relaxed.

Jet was attentive and she actually felt like

part of a couple. It was a good feeling. They still hadn't had a conversation about what the two of them were doing but the sparks were flying.

As the sun went down and the food was cleared away Dutchy picked up his guitar and started playing Christmas carols. Jet pulled Mei onto his lap as everyone joined in the singing. He snaked his arm around her hips and rested his chin on her shoulder. His breath was warm on her bare skin. She relaxed, happy to lean against him in the dark. It reminded her of the night they'd met. A warm summer's evening, music playing, the scent of frangipani in the air.

She could feel the heat of Jet's hand through the thin silk fabric of her dress. His hand slid down the side of her leg and under the hem of her skirt. She closed her eyes and pictured each fingertip where it rested on her thigh. Jet's thumb was making tiny, lazy circles on her skin and Mei stopped singing, focusing only on the sensation of his touch. She shifted in her seat, wanting more, until Jet's hand slowed and he whispered, 'Do you want to get out of here?'

'Now?'

She felt him nod.

'And go where?' She knew where his train of thought was heading; she could feel it. Her heart was thumping in her chest.

'This can go one of two ways,' he said. 'We can decide to pretend that we don't have chemistry and focus on working out how we are going to raise our daughter as single parents or we can explore the spark between us and see what happens.'

'And if it just fizzles out? What happens to An Na then?'

'Nothing happens to An Na. She still has two parents. She doesn't need to know about any of this. Not until we figure it out. What do you think?'

The logical part of Mei's brain had shut down. The part that told her she wasn't eighteen any more, the part that said she needed more than chemistry, the part that said she needed someone who could be a partner for her and a father for An Na. An equal. She wasn't after a bit of fun any more—at least that was what she thought—but her body was crying out for his touch. Right now, she didn't care if they only had one night. She would willingly take that over the alternative of nothing. She wanted to see what happened. She wanted to take that chance. She was older and wiser and she wasn't about to repeat her mistakes. This wasn't a spontaneous or rash decision—she had thought of almost nothing else since the moment Jet had reappeared in her life. If she passed it up, she knew she'd regret it and she had plenty of regrets in her past already.

She still thought she might be crazy, but she wasn't going to say no. Was she setting herself up to fail? She'd never tried anything without knowing she could do it before. And giving herself over to Jet, letting him have half the control was scary for her, but if anyone could make her relinquish control it was him. She wanted to give herself to him, to see if it was the same as before. She missed that feeling, that connection to another person. Had their relationship been just a teenage dream, a holiday romance? Or could they sustain it, develop it into something more? She wanted to know. She needed to know.

'Let's go,' she said.

CHAPTER EIGHT

'THIS IS NICER than I expected,' Mei said as Jet unlocked the front door and led her inside.

'Were you imagining the caravan? I have grown up a bit since then.'

The house was freshly painted with polished wooden floorboards and a new kitchen. Surfboards were racked on one wall of the living room but, other than that, it didn't overtly look like a bachelor pad.

'I didn't mind the caravan.' She smiled. 'I have some fond memories of that weekend.'

'Is that so?'

'But it seems like a lifetime ago,' she said as she followed him through the house.

'Let me see if I can jog your memory,' he replied as he pushed open the door to his bedroom and switched on a lamp. He reached for her hand but before he led her into his room he said, 'Are you sure about this, Mei?'

He had to know she wanted this as much as he did.

Mei nodded and stepped inside his room. He closed the door as her hands went to the side of her dress. She unzipped it and pushed the straps from her shoulders and he watched, mesmerised, as her dress slithered to the floor.

Automatically his eyes had followed the movement as gravity took hold and his gaze was now focused on her dress where it lay in a pool of black silk around her ankles. His eyes travelled up the length of her bare legs, long and brown, to her slim hips.

Through the lace of her panties he could see the dark triangle of hair at the junction of her thighs. His mouth was dry and his legs were shaky as all the blood in his body rushed south. A severe lack of oxygen to his brain had left him light-headed and had robbed him of the power of speech. But he could admire. So he did.

Mei was almost naked, and she was gorgeous. She was still thin, but she'd filled out nicely and had curves in all the right places. His gaze travelled higher, over her flat stomach and her round belly button to her small, bare breasts and erect nipples. She was perfect.

He could see the pulse beating at the base of her throat, her lips were parted, her mouth pink and soft, her eyes gleaming. She was stunning.

He remembered how comfortable she'd been in her skin when she was eighteen. How years of ballet had shown her what her body could do. How she'd shown him. He remembered how she'd wrapped her body around his, how soft she'd looked, but how strong she'd been.

She lifted her hands and removed the clip that held her hair in place. Her hair tumbled over her shoulders as she reached for his hands.

He was almost afraid to let her touch him. Afraid of losing control.

'I want this,' she said. 'I want you.'

Jet swallowed. There was only so much temptation he could stand. He forgot about his daughter. He forgot about Mei being a mother—he forgot about everything as desire took over. With one step he closed the gap that had opened between them.

Her hands were on his arms as his fingers cupped the curve of her bottom. He pulled her to him and bent his head. She tipped her face up to him and he closed his eyes as their lips met. Her lips were soft and sweet. He stroked her cheek with a thumb and her lips parted. Her mouth was warm as she pressed against him. He could feel his erection, hard and stiff, between them.

Mei's fingers flicked open the button on his shorts and he kicked off his shoes as she slid his shorts from his hips. Her hands slid under his shirt and he broke their kiss as he impatiently pulled his shirt over his head. Now they were both semi-naked.

He scooped her into his arms. Her skin was warm and so soft, and inches of her bare flesh pressed against him as he held her. She wrapped her arms around his neck as he carried her to the bed. One, two, three, four steps across the room until he could gently lay her down.

He ran his fingers up her thigh, cupping

the curve of her bottom. Mei closed her eyes and arched her hips, pushing herself closer to him. He bent his head and kissed her. She opened her mouth, joining them together as he slid her panties from under her, pulling them off in one smooth movement.

He ran his hand over her hip and up across her stomach. His fingers grazed her breast and he watched as her nipple peaked under his touch. She moaned softly and reached for him but he wasn't done yet. He was calm and excited all at once but he was in no hurry.

He pushed her hair off her shoulders and bent his head, flicking his tongue over one breast and sucking it into his mouth. He supported himself on one elbow while he used his other hand in tandem with his mouth, teasing her nipples until both were taut with desire. He slid his knee between her thighs, parting them as he straddled her. His right hand stayed cupped over her breast as he moved his mouth lower to kiss her stomach.

He took his hand from her breast and ran it up the smooth skin of the inside of her thigh. She moaned and thrust her hips towards him as her knees dropped further apart.

Jet put his head between her thighs. He put his hands under her bottom and lifted her to his mouth, supporting her there as his tongue darted inside her. She was slick and sweet and she moaned as he explored her inner sanctum with his tongue. He enjoyed oral sex, giving and receiving, and tonight was no exception.

Mei thrust her hips towards him again, urging him deeper. He slid his fingers inside her where she was wet and hot, her sex swollen with desire. His fingers worked in tandem with his tongue, making her pant, making her beg for more.

'Jet, please. I want you inside me.'

But he wasn't ready to stop. Not yet.

He knew she was close to climaxing and he wanted to bring her to orgasm like this. He wanted to taste it, to feel it.

He ignored her request as he continued to work his magic with his tongue, licking and sucking the swollen bud of her desire. He continued until Mei had forgotten her request, until she had forgotten everything except her own satisfaction.

'Yes, yes…oh, Jet, don't stop.'

He had no intention of stopping.

He heard her sharp little intake of breath and then she began to shudder.

'Yes. Oh, Jet.'

She buried her fingers in his hair and clamped her thighs around his shoulders as she came. Shuddering and gasping before she collapsed, relaxed and spent.

Mei felt as if she'd shattered into a thousand pieces and it took her a few moments to gather herself together again. It was years since she'd slept with anyone, but she'd had no reservations. Her body had responded to Jet's touch as if she'd known him for ever. It felt as if every cell in her body recognised him. As if he could bring them all to life simultaneously until she exploded. All her concerns had ceased to exist. There had been no room in her head for a single conscious thought. It was all she could do to remember how to breathe as Jet reminded her of how it felt to let go, of how it felt to be a woman.

And now it was his turn. This time Mei took charge. His boxer shorts came off with one tug of her hand and as his erection sprang free Mei's groin flooded with heat and she felt the wetness between her thighs. She spread her legs and straddled him. She cupped him and then encircled his shaft with her hand. It was thick and hard and warm and pulsed with a life of its own as she ran her hand up its length. She rolled her fingers over the end and coaxed the moisture from his body.

Jet gasped and his body trembled. 'In the drawer by the bed,' he panted, 'I have protection.'

Mei opened the drawer and found a condom. She tore open the packet and watched his beautiful face as she rolled the sheath onto him. His blue eyes darkened as she brought herself forward, raising herself up onto her knees before lowering herself down. Jet closed his eyes and sighed as she took his length inside her.

She lifted herself up again, and down, as Jet held onto her hips and started to time her thrusts, matching their rhythms together. Slow at first and then gradually faster. And faster. Mei tried to stay in charge, but she found it impossible to control her body. All she could think of was how good this felt and that she wanted more. And more.

'Oh, God, yes.'

'Keep going. Don't stop.'

And, just when she thought she couldn't stand it any longer, Jet shuddered and she could feel his release as he came inside her. She held her breath as she let herself go and her body shook with pleasure as his orgasm was joined by hers. Their timing couldn't have been better.

Mei rolled over, tender and spent, and lay along Jet's side. He wrapped his arm around her and she felt as though her every wish had just been granted and she had everything she could ever want or need as she lay in Jet's embrace.

An Na had been chattering non-stop all day about all things Christmas. About the school concert, about what present she might get from her dad and about the afternoon's visit to see Father Christmas. She was frenetically excited, but Mei could understand how she felt. Mei felt the same way, only she was getting in a flap because of Jet, not because of the season.

She could scarcely believe that they had slept together last night. Or that their love-making had been as good as she remembered it being. Often over the years she'd wondered if she was looking at that weekend through rose-coloured glasses. If she had imagined the connection, the pleasure, the sheer ec-stasy she had found in Jet's arms. She won-dered if she had made it up as a way to soften the blow of falling pregnant, if she'd pre-tended to herself that she hadn't been able to resist, that they'd been destined to meet, to have a child. That their fate had been sealed somewhere in time without their knowledge. If she could blame fate then it wasn't her na-ivety, or her stupidity that had got her preg-nant. She had been powerless. And after last night she knew she hadn't made it all up. She'd been powerless again.

It was almost as if Jet had a force field around him that drew her in. She couldn't fight it, she didn't want to fight it, and last night she'd relived that fateful weekend all over again. And she was now hoping and praying that she would get another chance. And another. She almost needed to pinch herself.

She kept her eyes peeled for Jet. She and An Na had come to the mall early to do some Christmas shopping and Jet was meeting them here after he finished work.

She could see his blond hair in the distance, above the crowd which had gathered to visit the department store Father Christmas. She'd sent him a text, letting him know they were in the queue, and her body responded as she watched him weave his way towards them. She could feel her tummy tremble and her pelvis throbbed slightly. Her sex was still a little swollen and tender after last night. She smiled to herself as she wondered what he'd say if she told him that. Would he be shocked?

Jet reached them and greeted An Na with a kiss before kissing Mei. She'd turned her cheek, not wanting to answer questions from An Na if she let him kiss her properly. If she let him kiss her like she wanted him to.

An Na stood in front of them in the queue and Jet had his hand on Mei's waist. He let it drop to her bottom and she leant in against him as he winked at her. She hummed Christmas carols as they waited for An Na's turn.

'Hello, An Na,' Father Christmas greeted them when they finally made it to the front of the queue, 'and who have you brought with you this year?'

'This is my mummy and my daddy.'

'And have they been good?'

'Mummy has. Daddy, have you been good?' An Na asked.

'I've tried my best.' Jet held his hand over his heart and answered with a smile.

'And what about you, An Na?'

'I've been *very* good.'

'And what would you like for Christmas?'

'I'd like Mummy and Daddy to get married.'

Mei gasped. 'I thought you wanted a surprise from Father Christmas, An Na?'

'That would be a surprise,' An Na replied.

'It might be a bit tricky to fit Mummy and Daddy and a wedding into my sleigh,' the jolly man said, 'so why don't I get my elves to mark down a surprise for you this year and we'll see what happens after that, okay? Now, are you ready for your photo?'

'Okay,' An Na replied. 'Mummy and Daddy, are you going to be in the photo too?' she asked as both her parents hung back.

Jet was the first to agree and he stood behind Mei and rested one hand on her hip. She liked the way it felt. She liked the weight, the warmth, the strength and the security.

Once the picture had been taken and the visit completed, all they had to do was wait for the photo to be checked and emailed to Mei.

'Can I go on one of the rides while we wait?' An Na asked, pointing at the carousel that was set up in the toy department of the store.

Mei and Jet moved to stand by the roundabout, watching as An Na chose her horse and climbed on. Mei reached into her handbag and handed Jet a ticket.

'What's this?' he asked.

'Your ticket for the Christmas concert this weekend. We had to reserve tickets so the school knows how many to expect.'

'It's this weekend?'

'Yes.'

'I've got an event in Port Macquarie on the weekend. It's a qualifying event for the World Championships.'

'This weekend?'

He nodded.

'Which day?'

'Saturday.'

'Oh, well, that's okay,' Mei said, relieved. 'The concert is on Friday. You can do both.'

'No, I can't. I'm leaving on Friday.'

'Can't you leave on Saturday?'

'It's a four-hour drive, just to get to Port Macquarie. The race starts at six in the morning and takes over four hours to complete. There's no way I can drive up in the middle of the night and then be fresh enough to compete.'

'So you'll miss her concert.'

'It looks that way.'

'But you promised her.'

'I didn't know when it was.'

'You should have asked,' Mei snapped. He shouldn't have agreed to the concert without checking the details. She couldn't believe he was letting An Na down already.

'I didn't think to ask,' he admitted, 'but there's nothing I can do.'

Mei was annoyed. She'd love to have no responsibilities. She'd love to be able to chase her dreams. 'What's more important? Your race or An Na's concert?'

'I can't change the race.'

'And I can't change the concert.'

'But she'll have other concerts. This race is important.'

'So is An Na. I thought you said you didn't want her to feel like you don't have time for her. This concert is important; she is so excited that you are coming. I can't believe you're going to let her down. Having kids means that your plans change at the drop of a hat. You have to be flexible. You can't put yourself first.'

'Mei, you're not being fair. There's nothing I can do.'

Mei was close to tears. All the joy and delight from the past twenty-four hours evaporated in the space of a few minutes and one argument and it was obvious Jet was not budging. Their bond was tenuous and she could feel it starting to unravel under the weight of the disagreement but if he wasn't going to prioritise his daughter she didn't know what she could do about it.

'You'll have to tell her that you can't make it,' she said.

What did this mean for their future as a little family? Would he always have other priorities? She was juggling motherhood, a career and helping her parents in the restaurant. His life revolved around training commitments.

Had he been right when he'd said he worried about not being father material? It was obvious he didn't get it.

'Bondi Eleven, we've got a call for assistance at Ben Buckler.'

'This is Bondi Eleven, go ahead,' Poppy responded.

'We've had a report of a person on the rocks at Ben Buckler. Bondi lifeguards have requested assistance.'

'We're on our way,' Poppy replied as she started the ambulance.

'Who or what or where is Ben Buckler?' Mei asked as she clicked her seatbelt into position. It didn't sound as if the dispatcher was going to give any more information about the location.

'It's the area at the northern end of Bondi Beach. Near the golf course. Have you not been there before?'

'No. Should I have?'

'It where the big cliffs are.'

'Oh.' Now she knew where Poppy was talking about. 'You get a lot of calls for help out there?'

Poppy nodded.

'The person on the rocks—they're talking about the base of the cliffs?' Mei asked. She could imagine the type of incidents that would occur there.

'Yes. It's a popular spot for rock climbers. Most of these calls usually involve a mishap with one of them, rather than anything more dramatic or mental health related, although we get those too.'

Mei relaxed and hoped that was the case today. She hoped the outcome wasn't going to be disastrous or tragic. But the location presented other challenges. The cliffs were high and imposing and access would be difficult.

'How do we get down to the bottom?'

'That depends. Obviously, we can't get down there—it would need the special ops team—so the lifeguards usually go in from the water.'

'The lifeguards will do the retrieval?' She wondered if she would see Jet. They hadn't spoken since their disagreement at the department store and she had no idea if they were going to be able to get past that.

'If they can. Sometimes Lifeguard One is called in.'

'Lifeguard One?'

'The helicopter. We're just on standby really; we wait and see what the situation is and what decision is made regarding retrieval. If the person's injuries aren't serious, and the lifeguards can extract them using the jet ski and rescue mat, we'll meet them at the beach. If it's more serious than that the helicopter team will come into play. We'll go to the headland first though, so we can get a handle on what's happening.'

A crowd had gathered by the time they

reached the headland. Poppy and Mei got out of the ambulance as the jet ski rounded the base of the cliffs. Ryder was driving the ski and Mei could see Jet on the back.

There was a body on the rocks. Immobile. 'How will they reach the patient?' Mei asked.

'Jet will jump off the ski and get onto the rocks.'

'He'll do what!?'

Waves crashed onto the rocks. Mei knew they would be slippery underfoot and she couldn't imagine how Jet could safely negotiate his way from the ski to the base of the cliff. 'Isn't that dangerous?

'Jet knows what he's doing,' Poppy reassured her. 'He can read the ocean and the swell—his years of surfing experience will hold him in good stead. He'll be okay.'

Mei's heart was in her mouth as she watched Ryder time the swell of the ocean and she saw Jet leap from the ski. She had her hands clasped tightly and she held her breath, but somehow Jet landed safely on the rocks.

She breathed a sigh of relief as he moved

away from the edge, away from the impact zone where the waves were still crashing onto the rocks. At least now she didn't have to worry about him getting swept off and into the ocean.

He scrambled across the rocks and knelt beside the patient.

'Now what?' she asked.

'Now we wait. Jet will assess the patient and determine the extent of his injuries and make a decision about evacuation.'

Poppy was holding the radio from the ambulance and it crackled to life as the communications centre relayed the information Jet was reporting to the tower.

'Male, age thirty-two, fell while rock climbing. Bilateral simple ankle fractures.'

'He's not walking out of there,' Poppy said as they heard the call go out to Lifeguard One.

'So that's us done? We're not needed?' Mei raised her voice to be heard as the helicopter flew overhead but her voice wobbled with fear. The patient had been safely extracted but Jet was still at the base of the cliffs, alone on the slippery rocks, and Ryder was sitting on the jet ski fifty or so metres out to sea. Somehow Jet had to get off the rocks and back to the beach. She might be annoyed with him but she didn't want any misfortune to happen to him.

Poppy nodded. 'We'll just wait and make sure Jet gets back out to Ryder, but we're done. Are you okay?'

No, Mei was far from okay. She was extremely anxious. Her hands were tightly clenched together and her heart was racing.

She shook her head. 'I'm worried about Jet and I'm not sure if I should be.'

'He'll be fine; he knows what he's doing and this spot isn't as dangerous as it looks. He'll come back to you, safe and sound.'

'That's partly what I'm worried about.'

Poppy frowned. 'I'm not following you.'

'I'm worried for his safety, of course, but I know he understands the water. Far better than he understands me or me him. That's what concerns me. That he won't come back to me. That he's not interested in being a father or in having a relationship with me.'

'And you are?'

Mei nodded. 'I've never got over him.

When I bumped into him again here I thought maybe my feelings were so strong because of An Na and the connection I felt through her to Jet, but it's more than that. It's much deeper. But his priorities are very different to mine—too different. I fear for us to be able to find some middle ground. For us to find our way to each other with any sort of permanence.'

'And that's what you want?' Poppy asked as they watched Jet dive off the rocks into the ocean and swim out to where Ryder waited on the jet ski.

Mei nodded. 'For me and for An Na. But I think Jet and I are on completely different wavelengths and I don't get the sense that he is ready to take on a serious relationship. He seems caught up in his solitary bachelor life and his training and I don't think he has room for me or wants to make room. He's trying with An Na, I get that, but I want him to try harder and I'm worried that this little bit of him that we're getting is all he can give. I'm worried I'm wishing for something that is impossible.'

'Have you told him how you feel?'

Mei shook her head as they returned to the ambulance. 'I think we've got enough on our plates with figuring An Na out without complicating it. I can't demand something of him that he can't give me.'

'But you like him?'

Mei nodded.

'Maybe you need to take the first step. Tell him how you feel. Our family isn't great at expressing our emotions. I know he's besotted with An Na and I've seen the way he looks at you.'

'How?'

'Like you are the sun, the moon and the stars. Like you're precious and delicate and he can't believe you're real. Give him a chance. He isn't great at communicating and I know he's worried about his ability to be a good father. We didn't grow up in a conventional family and none of us really know if we've got the skills to raise a family of our own. You'll have to teach him.'

'I don't know if he's ready to learn. I'm scared there are too many hurdles for us to get over.'

'Be patient. It's a big adjustment. But he's

a good guy. He's loyal and kind but he needs something, someone, to anchor him. Not to tether him or tie him down but someone he can rely on to be there when things don't go his way and who will celebrate the successes with him. Someone who will be proud of him and support him. Our parents weren't like that.'

Mei's family had always been there for her. Even when she fell pregnant they stood by her. She knew they would never abandon her.

'Jet has always had our support, but he needs more. He needs you,' Poppy said as she started the engine. 'He needs encouragement and attention. He's afraid of being rejected if he fails. He needs to know you'll be there for him no matter what. If you can give him that you'll reap the rewards.'

Mei wasn't sure she and Jet would be able to make this work but she vowed to be more supportive. One of them had to act like a grown-up and perhaps she was being unfair, expecting him to drop everything and change his life because of a decision she'd made eight years ago.

She wished she could turn off her feelings

but she couldn't. He made her giddy, nervous and excited and she didn't want to let go of that. Not without a fight. If she wanted to make this work, maybe she needed to heed Poppy's advice.

CHAPTER NINE

MEI HAD MADE a promise to herself that she would be patient, that she would be support-ive, but she found it hard to remember her promise when An Na's Christmas concert was ten minutes from starting and not only was Jet absent but she knew he hadn't told An Na about his schedule clash. She was fu-rious that he was going to let her down. That he was going to let them both down.

She had delayed going into the school hall, hoping in vain that Jet might still turn up, but she could see the hall was nearing capacity. Su-Lin and Bo were saving her a seat in the second row and if she didn't claim it soon other parents would have it in their sights.

She bit back her frustration. She was dis-appointed in Jet, disappointed for An Na, disappointed for herself. She was being a romantic, dreaming of a future that wasn't going to happen. Surely it was better to know now.

She wiped a tear from the corner of her eye, straightened her shoulders and pasted a smile on her face. She didn't want to ruin An Na's day any further by letting her daughter see her cry. She would smile and enjoy the concert even if she felt like screaming. The person she wanted to scream at was God knew where and it wasn't fair to take her frustrations out on anyone else.

She excused herself as she side-stepped past other parents and took her seat beside Su-Lin. Her sister-in-law reached across and squeezed her hand in support as the school's principal stepped on stage. Mei did her best to ignore the empty seat on her left, the one Su-Lin had optimistically kept for Jet.

'You okay?' Su-Lin asked.

'Not really.'

Poppy had told her she needed to give Jet time. People kept telling her what Jet needed, but were any of them giving him advice? Were any of them telling him what *she* needed? That she wanted someone to step up and share the responsibility of parenting. She didn't want someone who was only prepared to do the fun stuff, the surfing lessons and the visits to Father Christmas. She wanted someone to help with the boring, mundane but important day-to-day stuff too. She needed someone on her side.

Mei could feel the tension in her jaw and shoulders and she tried to relax as the principal introduced An Na's class. She smiled as her daughter came onto the stage and soon discovered that watching An Na's enthusiastic performance was the perfect thing to distract her from the thoughts relentlessly swirling around in her head. She even managed to make it through the pieces and songs that the other classes presented.

She knew she was biased but she thought An Na was brilliant. She sang carols with her class before she and some of her friends who attended the same ballet classes performed a dance. Mei clapped and smiled as the little girls finished their routine. An Na did a half-curtsey and waved to Mei, but her attention was quickly diverted and Mei saw her waving towards the rear of the hall. She turned in her seat to see who had caught her daughter's attention and her heart skipped a beat when she saw Jet leaning against the back wall. What on earth was he doing here? Had he cancelled his plans? Was he putting An Na first?

She fidgeted through the last few performances, wishing they would be over, wanting to go to Jet. Her concentration was completely shot and all she could think about was making a beeline for him to find out what was going on. What had made him change his mind.

The entire junior school was on stage to sing the final carol and as soon as they filed off Mei was ready to spring to her feet. But as the applause died down the principal came back onto the stage with her final message and Mei sank back into her chair. Would this never end?

At last the audience was excused. Mei stood and turned towards the back of the hall, but her view was now obscured by all the other parents. She had no chance of seeing over people's heads; her line of sight was level with people's chests. The parents on her left were in no hurry to move and Mei didn't want to push past them again, but if they didn't hurry and gather their belongings she would have no choice.

Finally, they began to move and she was almost treading on their heels in her haste to get out of the row.

'I'll meet you outside,' she told Su-Lin. If her sister-in-law wondered where the fire was she didn't say.

Mei dodged and weaved past the dawdling parents but when she eventually made it to the back of the hall Jet was nowhere to be seen. She stepped outside and scanned the grounds but there was no sign of him. She knew she hadn't imagined his presence so where was he?

'Mummy! Mummy! Did you like my dancing?'

Mei almost overbalanced as An Na came running towards her and threw her arms around her waist. She scooped her up and took a step backwards, regaining her feet as she smiled at her daughter. 'I thought you were magnificent,' she told her. 'I loved it.'

'Did you see Daddy?' An Na asked as she set her back down on the ground.

So she *hadn't* imagined him. That eased her mind. She nodded. 'I did.'

'Look what he gave me.'

An Na's fingers were at her neck. She was holding a delicate silver chain between her thumb and forefinger and Mei could see a tiny charm hanging from the chain. She squatted down to get a closer look. It was a girl on a surfboard.

'It's me!' An Na exclaimed.

'I can see that,' Mei replied and wondered why Jet was buying An Na gifts this close to Christmas. She knew she was looking for flaws in his behaviour and she didn't like the way that made her feel about herself. She saw Su-Lin heading towards them and she held up one finger and motioned 'one minute' to her as she took out her phone. She needed to speak to Jet.

'Hi, where are you?' she asked as he answered her call.

'In the car on the way to Port Macquarie.'

Mei frowned. 'But I saw you at the concert.'

'Yes. And now I'm in the car.'

'But we're going out for pizza.'

'Mei…' She heard him sigh. 'No one said anything about pizza and I couldn't stay. I shouldn't have stayed for the concert, but Ryder offered to drive me up the coast tonight and I thought I could make it work.'

'Can't you leave in the morning?' She hated the fact that she was almost begging when really she should be thanking him for being there for An Na, but the words were out before she could stop herself.

'I've changed my plans once already and no, I can't go in the morning, the race starts at six am. As it is, I should have been up there tonight to prepare. Ryder is driving me so I can sleep in the car. It's not ideal preparation but a promise is a promise and I didn't want to let An Na down.' He paused and she knew he was waiting for her to respond. Waiting for her to say it was okay, but the words stuck in her throat. She wanted him there. With An Na. With her. 'Mei, I don't know what else you want from me. It seems like nothing I do is good enough.'

He'd done the right thing by An Na, he'd

watched her concert as he'd promised, and Mei knew this shouldn't be about her, it *wasn't* about her, except that she wished it was. She wished she was a priority for Jet too.

Mei nibbled on a shortbread biscuit that An Na and Daisy had baked and sipped her champagne as she watched Lily and An Na decorate the Christmas tree. She was tired and on edge, wound tight from lack of sleep and stress. She'd spent the past few days re-hashing her post-concert conversation with Jet and thinking of all the ways it could have gone differently. And now he was back from Port Macquarie but things between them had definitely not improved. The tension was pal-pable and the air frosty.

Jet had come fourth in his race and Mei was feeling guilty. He had needed to finish second or higher to get automatic selection into the national team for the World Cham-pionships and Mei couldn't help wondering if he'd stuck to his original plan and trav-elled to Port Macquarie the day before the race, rather than arriving at the last minute, he would have been better rested and the result could have been different. He hadn't said anything to her about the race but she knew he was disappointed and was now pinning all his hopes on the final qualifying event which was being held four days after Christmas in Bondi.

Jet had barely spoken to her. For once she had no idea what he was thinking. Was he annoyed or upset with her? Did he think she was too demanding? Unreasonable? Or was he simply upset about the race? She knew he'd been surprised to see her here, but he hadn't questioned her presence, but still, she needed to get him alone. They needed to talk but he was doing his best to avoid her.

Mei appreciated that Jet's sisters seemed determined to try to fix things between their brother and her. She knew that was why Lily had invited her and An Na to join them today, to help decorate the Christmas tree. Lily had explained it was her tradition, albeit a relatively recent one that had begun when she'd married and moved into this house, but whichever of her siblings were in Sydney were always invited to help decorate the tree.

An Na could have gone alone but Lily had insisted that she come too, and Mei didn't have the heart to suggest that their efforts to mend bridges would be in vain. Jet was proud and Mei knew she would have to fix this.

She looked up at the tree as she finished the shortbread. It was looking festive and she was hoping the sight of the tree would lift her spirits a little and restore some Christmas cheer. Lily had chosen a blue and silver theme this year, which Mei had to admit had surprised her at first. Her family celebrated Christmas too but their decorations had always stuck to the traditional red. She wondered if that was a throwback to her parents' youth, growing up in Hong Kong under British governance, or if it was because the Chinese associated the colour red with good luck and fortune. She'd never thought about it before but she liked the idea of choosing a theme. And the blue and silver made it feel like a fresh start, a new beginning.

Maybe she wouldn't get quite the new beginning she'd been hoping for, but if An Na could get to know her father and be happy that was enough for Mei. She would learn to be content with that.

Jet was lifting An Na up so she could place the angel at the top of the tree when Lily's phone rang. He might have been avoiding Mei but his attitude towards An Na was unchanged and for that she was grateful. Jet might want nothing to do with her but it looked as if he intended to keep his promise to be a part of An Na's life.

Mei was watching Jet and An Na but she could see Lily too and her attention was caught when she saw Lily freeze. She went absolutely still as the blood drained from her face.

'Lily, what is it? What's wrong?' Mei crossed the room and made Lily sit down; she looked as if she might faint. 'Who's on the phone?'

'Mum,' Lily said as she ended the call.

Mei saw Poppy's head swivel towards them. 'What did she want?'

'Dad is in hospital.' Lily was looking at her siblings but Mei could tell she wasn't really seeing them. 'He's in a coma.'

'What?' Daisy asked. 'What happened?' she asked.

Everything came to a stop as they all waited to hear what Lily had to say. 'It sounds like he's had a ruptured brain aneurysm.'

That wasn't good. Mei looked around the room, waiting for someone to say something, but all four of the siblings were silent. She assumed they were in shock and she knew someone needed to take charge.

'He's in Byron Bay?' she asked.

'Yes,' Jet replied as he handed An Na another piece of shortbread.

Mei wanted to yell at him, to tell him this was no time for shortbread.

'Okay, so what do we need to do? How will we get you all there?' she asked.

'Where?'

'To Byron, to see your father.'

'Why?'

'What do you mean "why"? Your father is critically ill; you need to go to see him.'

'We'll have to drive,' Lily said, coming out of her trance. 'Who's going to come?'

Mei frowned. Why would Lily ask who

was going? Why would that be up for discussion? Surely, they would all be going.

'I'll come with you,' Daisy said.

'Poppy?'

'I guess so.'

What was wrong with this family?

'Jet?'

'I'm supposed to be taking An Na surfing tomorrow.'

'Don't be ridiculous,' Mei told him. 'That doesn't matter. Your father is much more important.'

Jet was shaking his head. 'He doesn't need me there. We don't have a close relationship.'

'Jet, you need to go with your sisters,' Mei insisted. 'If you don't want to be there for your dad you should at least go to support your mum.'

'She doesn't need us either. Our family is not like yours, Mei. Goldie doesn't need us—she only ever needed our father. He is her world.'

'All the more reason for you to go then,' Mei said. 'He's in hospital. She doesn't have him to lean on. She will need you.'

'You can't have it both ways, Mei.' Jet's

tone was abrupt and Mei felt it slice through her like a knife to the heart.

'I think you should take your discussion out to the deck,' Lily interrupted. 'Away from little ears.'

Jet and Mei both looked towards An Na before heeding Lily's warning.

'What do you mean, "both ways"?' Mei asked as they stepped outside.

'One minute you're telling me I'm not prioritising An Na, I'm not committing to my promises, that I'm not meeting your expectations of what a proper father should be, and the next telling me your family doesn't matter.'

'I was talking about a surfing lesson,' Mei replied. 'A surfing lesson can wait. Your family has to come first.'

'But a few days ago you thought my race could wait. Why do you get to decide what is and isn't important?'

'Is that what this is all about? You're blaming me for what happened in the race?'

'No. I'm blaming myself for that. But it seems that, no matter what I do, it's never enough for you. Never the right thing. I don't know what you want from me but I'm beginning to suspect that I will continue to disappoint you, that I cannot be the man you want me to be. And perhaps we need to think about that.'

'You okay?' Jet asked Poppy as they sat outside the critical care unit of the Byron Bay hospital. The drive from Sydney had taken eight hours and it was late in the day, but they had gone straight to the hospital and were now waiting for their mother to come out and give them some information about Pete's condition.

'I don't know,' Poppy replied. 'I haven't seen Mum or Dad for a year, and it feels strange to be waiting to see them in a hospital. Dad always seemed so fit and healthy. I know these things happen out of the blue, I've seen it often enough in my job, but it just isn't making sense. I'm a bit out of whack, but I'll be okay. It's you I'm worried about.'

'Me?'

Poppy nodded. 'Things seem a little strained between you and Mei. What's going on there?'

'I'm not really sure, to be honest. This is all new to me and I feel like I'm constantly mucking things up. I know we think Mum and Dad didn't do a great job of raising us, but bringing up a kid is harder than I thought.'

'You're doing well with An Na. You're a natural with kids and she adores you.'

'Maybe.' Jet shrugged. 'But I'm not doing so well with Mei. She's got high expectations and I want to live up to them but I'm not sure that I can.'

'Perhaps, when we get home, the two of you need to sit down and have a proper discussion about your goals and expectations. About what your future looks like.'

The idea of that terrified Jet. He knew he would fail to live up to Mei's expectations. But wouldn't it be better to fail Mei than to fail An Na? As much as the thought of that conversation terrified him, he knew Poppy was right. There was no avoiding the fact that they needed to talk, and he was about to agree with Poppy just as their mother emerged from the CCU.

Jet got a shock when he saw Goldie. Like

Poppy, it was over a year since he'd visited and Goldie, who was only forty-eight and usually looked younger, appeared to have aged ten years.

Lily stood up and went to hug her. Jet, Poppy and Daisy stayed in their seats. Goldie seemed dazed. She let Lily hug her but she didn't return the hug. Her arms hung limply at her sides.

'I don't understand how this happened,' Goldie said as Lily released her. 'Pete is fit. He'd been surfing. I don't understand.'

'Mum—' Lily put her hands on Goldie's shoulders and forced her to make eye contact '—tell me what happened.'

'He'd been surfing and complained of a headache. He collapsed on the beach and was brought to hospital.'

'What has the doctor said?'

'The doctor?' Goldie repeated. 'I don't know.'

'Did they say anything about surgery?'

'I can't remember. He might have said something about draining fluid.'

Lily turned to her siblings. 'Stay with Mum. I'll go and find someone to talk to.'

They waited in silence for a while but when Lily didn't return Jet started asking questions.

'How does this happen, Poppy? What causes it?' he asked.

'It can be genetic,' Poppy said, 'and can also be related to illness or drug use, but often there's no specific cause. You can have aneurysms that never burst—they just sit there and you wouldn't know they existed.'

'I've spoken to the surgeon,' Lily said when she came back. 'He's put a catheter in to drain the fluid off Dad's brain. He's recovered consciousness but the next twenty-four hours are critical. There's a high risk of another bleed in that time frame. They want to operate.'

'Operate? On his brain?'

Lily nodded. 'They have two options. In one they insert a catheter through an artery in the groin and then push a soft wire through that into the aneurysm and seal it off. In the other they remove a section of skull and clip the aneurysm directly to stop the blood flow.'

'They cut open his skull?'

'Yes.'

'Will they do that here?'

'No, they need to move him to Brisbane and there are risks associated with both options.'

'What sort of risks?'

'Post-op pulmonary oedema is the biggest concern. That can cause heart attacks. The surgeon has spoken to Dad about his options; he's going to discuss it with Mum but he wants to see each of us one by one first.'

'Who does? The surgeon?'

'No, Dad. He's conscious.'

Jet sat and waited as his sisters each had their turn. The hospital was decorated for Christmas and it seemed completely surreal to be sitting outside the critical care unit surrounded by tinsel and sparkling lights.

'Your turn,' Poppy said as she emerged from the unit. Her eyes were red and Jet was surprised to see her upset. Of his three sisters, Poppy was the most self-contained. Lily and Daisy were far more emotional. Had Pete said something or was his condition really critical? Lily had said there were surgical options and Jet had just assumed that meant it was a problem that could be fixed. Had he misunderstood? What were they really dealing with? What was he walking into?

He was dreading what was about to happen. He wasn't ready to deal with this. It was way beyond his emotional experience. His heart was racing and his palms were sweating. He knew it was anxiety. Nervousness he could handle. He was nervous before a race but he'd learned to use that surge of adrenalin to focus his body and mind on the physical effort that awaited him. He'd trained for those situations but today was something new. He was unprepared—woefully unprepared—and he felt certain it was going to be a disaster. He was bound to say the wrong thing or have nothing to say. Which would be better? Which would be worse?

His thoughts turned to Mei. She'd know how to calm him down, to focus his thoughts, and she'd know what to say to Pete too. Jet was completely lost.

He wished Mei was with him. But she wasn't. He was on his own.

He wiped his hands on his shorts, trying to get rid of the clamminess. He took a deep breath, stood up, pushed open the door and stepped into the unknown.

His father was blond and tanned, an older version of his son, and he looked incongruous lying in a hospital bed. If it wasn't for the tubes protruding from him and the leads connecting him to the machines, he would have looked perfectly fine.

He was awake.

Jet knew he should be pleased that his father was conscious, that he had survived, but all he could think of was that now he would have to make conversation and he and his father hadn't had a proper conversation for fifteen years.

He stopped himself from asking Pete how he was feeling. It would have been a ridiculous question, given the circumstances. He sat beside the bed and said the first thing that came to mind. 'I hear you've got a trip to Brisbane coming up.'

'Yeah, never much cared for the city.'

'Well, I expect they'll fix you up and send you back here as quick as they can.'

'I hope so but, in case they don't, in case

something goes wrong, there are some things I need to say to you.'

Jet had not prepared himself for a personal discussion. He'd already forgotten, or chosen to ignore, the fact that Pete had asked to speak to each of his children individually. That should have served as a warning, but Jet and his father had never shared their thoughts and feelings. They had spent time together in the waves, but surfing hadn't involved much communication. And that was the way they both liked it.

'You don't need to rest?'

'No,' Pete said. 'I'm about to put my life in the hands of some doctor I don't know, things might not go according to plan and there are some things I want to say that I might not get a chance to say later. I need to get this off my chest. I need to apologise.'

'What for?'

'For not spending more time with you. I feel that I don't really know you and I'm sorry about that. And now, faced with my own mortality, I realise I might never get that chance. Before today I would have blamed my own parents for the way I brought you all up, but the blame stops with me. Raising you kids the way we did was a conscious decision on my part. Along with your mother. My parents were strict, my father in particular was very demanding, and I vowed not to bring you kids up the same way. I wasn't going to insist you follow our rules or chase our dreams.

'My parents insisted I study medicine. I wasn't at all interested but that was what all the men in my family did and it was expected of me too. I hated it. I failed second year and then dropped out. I went travelling and ended up here, where I met your mother. Once I met Goldie, that was it. I wasn't going anywhere. And we've been together ever since. I don't regret that but what I do regret is that I didn't set goals for myself. I always thought I would have time to do things later, but the opportunities weren't available in Byron back then. I ended up with the surf shop and surf school. I love that job, but I do wonder if I could have done more, accomplished more. It's too late for me now, but I'm really proud of you kids and what you've achieved.'

Jet didn't feel that he'd achieved very much

yet—not compared to his sisters. He believed he could do it but he realised now that he needed someone else to believe in him, to make him try harder. He needed someone to impress, someone to be proud of him. He needed a reason to set an example, a reason to do his best, and Mei had given him that reason. He would try, not just for An Na but for Mei as well. She had achieved so much as a single mother—her career, raising a daughter—and Jet realised he needed to step up and show her that he had what it took. That she could rely on him, that he wouldn't give up.

'I didn't want to pressure you kids like I'd been pressured,' Pete said. 'I figured we'd give you freedom to make your own decisions, your own mistakes.'

'Kids need boundaries,' Jet said. He hadn't known that, growing up. He'd revelled in the freedom he'd been given, but as he'd become an adult and interacted with the lifeguards and their families and with the teenagers on Bondi, he'd learned the value of boundaries. Growing up in the commune, they'd had no restrictions and Jet now knew that his life could have gone in a whole different direction. He'd been a wild teenager who could have so easily gone off the rails.

'I know. But I wanted to give you space. I wanted to be your friend, not your father. I probably needed to find a happy medium, but I didn't want to turn out like my father. You'll probably say the same one day.'

It wasn't that Jet was desperate not to be like him, but he wanted to do a better job than his father had done.

'That's what worries me, that I—probably all of us, but me in particular—won't know how to parent. How to show love and affection but still set boundaries, how to encourage without spoiling, how to discipline without damaging.'

'It sounds like you are already a step ahead of where your mother and I were. All I could think about were the things I didn't want to do, not what I should do. And Goldie had even less idea than I did about how to raise a family. She'd never had an example set. She was raised in foster homes and ran away at eighteen and when she fell pregnant she didn't know what she was doing and neither did I. If it wasn't for everyone in the commune rallying around us we wouldn't have survived. It took us a long time to work things out. Goldie kept getting pregnant and she was never emotionally equipped to deal with the hard aspects of raising kids. We put each other first when we should have prioritised you kids. I feel like we've let you down and I'm sorry. But, despite all our mistakes, you're doing well and I am proud of you. I wish I could say we helped. I know you'll do a better job when it's your turn.'

'It's my turn now.' Jet hadn't meant to say that. He'd had no intention of divulging anything personal to his father, but An Na and Mei had been in his thoughts since he'd arrived in Byron Bay and he'd spoken without thinking.

'What do you mean?'

'I have a seven-year-old daughter.'

'I have a granddaughter? And you never thought to tell us? You never thought we'd like to meet her?'

'I didn't know about her,' he said. 'I've only just met her, but no, I didn't think about introducing her to you. I didn't think you'd be interested.' He knew he sounded harsh, but it was the truth. Introducing An Na to his sisters was one thing, meeting his parents was something else altogether. But, once again, he could hear Mei's voice in his head and he knew what her opinion would be. She would insist at some point that An Na meet her paternal grandparents, but he'd worry about that another day.

Right now, he knew that he would do whatever it took to ensure he didn't let An Na down.

As he sat by his father's hospital bed, he promised himself and An Na that he wouldn't make the same mistakes. An Na didn't need a buddy; she needed guidance, boundaries and love. He would be involved; he would make sure she knew she was loved.

Mei was doing a brilliant job but he needed to step up for both Mei and An Na. His daughter had one parent but she needed two. She deserved two.

Being a parent wasn't necessarily harder than he'd thought; he'd always thought it would be difficult and that he wasn't cut out for it, but that was irrelevant now. He was a parent, and it was his responsibility to be the best he could be and he vowed to do a better job than his father had.

He could do better. He *would* do better.

He didn't want to be a part-time father, and he didn't want An Na looking to anyone else for a parental figure. It had to be him and he didn't want to be without Mei. He wanted to raise An Na with Mei. He was determined to be a father and a husband and that meant he had to set the wheels in motion to sort out how they were going to live their life. What his life—their life—was going to look like going forward.

He needed to put An Na and Mei first.

People didn't always get a second chance—he hadn't really even had a first chance with An Na or Mei—and he now knew exactly what he was going to do.

CHAPTER TEN

'MUMMY, MUMMY, LOOK, it's Father Christmas!'

Mei had been watching the beach, looking for Jet, when An Na began excitedly pointing out to sea. Jet had asked them to meet him on Bondi Beach at the end of his shift but when Mei arrived at the lifeguard tower Ryder had directed her down to the sand. She hadn't been able to see Jet anywhere on the beach and was wondering if he had made a mistake, but as she turned to look out to the ocean she realised Jet wasn't missing and Ryder wasn't mistaken.

An Na was right. Father Christmas was out on the water. To be exact, Father Christmas was coming towards them on a jet ski, standing up as he rode in to the shore, and there was something very familiar about the way he stood and the tilt of his head. Despite the costume, Mei knew instantly that it was Jet. What she didn't know was why he was dressed in a red suit, white beard and sunglasses and why he was balancing an enormous present under his left arm.

An Na was tugging on her hand, pulling her down to the water's edge as Jet guided the watercraft into the shallows and came to a stop.

'Ho, ho, ho, Merry Christmas!' he said as he leapt from the ski, wrestling with the present at the same time.

It was late afternoon on Christmas Eve but there were still plenty of families enjoying the perfect summer weather and An Na and Mei had been joined by dozens of other children, all eager to see Father Christmas.

The lifeguard buggy pulled up behind them and Dutchy and Ryder jumped out. They were wearing Christmas hats and their lifeguard shorts and they each carried large red sacks.

Jet had the present he'd brought with him tucked under one arm. It was wrapped in red and white Christmas paper and shaped suspiciously like a surfboard. He put it into the back of the buggy and picked up another sack and proceeded to hand out individually wrapped chocolates and lollies to the crowd of children, assisted by Dutchy and Ryder.

Mei smiled as she watched the proceedings; she thought the lifeguards were having as much fun as the children.

An Na still hadn't recognised Jet but once the children dispersed, munching on their sweets, Jet removed his beard.

'Daddy!' An Na clapped her hands and ran to hug him. 'What are you doing?'

'I'm helping Father Christmas. He's got a busy day tomorrow, so I thought I'd help him get a head start. He gave me something for you.'

'What is it?'

'I think it's a surprise. Do you want to see?'

An Na was hopping from one foot to the other. 'Yes!'

He took her over to the buggy and lifted the parcel out, standing it upright on the sand.

'This is for me?' An Na's eyes were wide.

Jet nodded and held the top of the present as An Na started to rip the paper from the gift.

'It's a surfboard! Is it really mine? Mummy, look, a surfboard!'

'It's fantastic, isn't it, darling?' Mei pasted a smile on her face. She'd known what it was—it was pretty hard to disguise a surfboard—but part of her was a little miffed that Jet hadn't discussed the gift with her because she knew his present was going to outshine hers. Although she couldn't deny he'd been quite clever, gifting it from Father Christmas, and seeing the delight on An Na's face she knew she couldn't begrudge the fact that Jet had chosen the perfect gift for their daughter.

But she couldn't help feeling that he was still getting to do all the fun stuff, the lighter side of parenting. She was still the disciplinarian, the one who figured out the day-to-day needs of her daughter—their daughter—and she was tired of doing it alone.

But she had to give him some credit. He hadn't abandoned them. He was trying.

She remembered Poppy's advice. She

needed to give him time. She did owe him that. Finding out he was a father would have been a massive shock and to his credit he hadn't run away. It wasn't his fault that he coped with humour—that he didn't seem to be taking it seriously. That was her perception. She hadn't asked him how he was coping—she'd been too wrapped up in her own thoughts, her own needs. He deserved better than that. She needed to lighten up.

She knew she overthought things. She knew she could be too serious. Maybe she should take a leaf out of his book. The world wasn't going to end if she relaxed a little and gave him some space. Maybe she was asking for too much. She kept saying that all she wanted was for An Na to be happy and she was. Perhaps, with time, Mei could be happy too, but for now she'd try to relax, she'd try not to overthink things. She'd do her best not to expect too much or berate Jet for not meeting her expectations. She could admit that perhaps her expectations had been unrealistic. Time would tell, and in the meantime Jet didn't look as if he was going anywhere. Maybe things would still be okay.

'I love it!' An Na said as she let go of the board and threw her arms around Jet again. 'And I love you.'

'I love you too, my gorgeous girl.'

Mei caught her breath. She hadn't heard Jet tell An Na that he loved her before. She lifted one hand and wiped a tear from her eye, pleased that Jet and An Na were too pre-occupied to notice her sentimentality.

What would he say if she told him she loved him? Was he ready to hear that? Was she ready to tell him?

She knew she loved him. Why hadn't she told him?

She knew it was because she was afraid that he wouldn't say it back. That he wasn't ready, that he might *never* be ready, and she couldn't take that rejection. While she kept silent she could keep the dream alive.

'You okay?'

Ryder was standing beside her. Mei nod-ded. She was overcome with emotion, which robbed her of speech as she wondered if Jet would ever say those words to her.

'Can we go surfing now?' An Na asked.

'In a minute, sweetheart,' Jet replied. 'I just need to ask your mum something.'

'I can take you, An Na,' Ryder offered. 'I have officially finished work for the day.'

Mei could tell An Na was torn between wanting Jet to take her and wanting to get into the water as soon as possible. 'That's a good idea, An Na,' she encouraged. She was keen to know what Jet wanted.

Ryder took off his Christmas hat and tossed it into the buggy when An Na agreed to let him surf with her. An Na was already in her bathers; Mei suspected she would spend the entire summer in swimwear and in the ocean with Jet if she had half a chance. Ryder picked up An Na's new board and the two of them headed into the surf. Jet stripped off his costume, leaving him bare-chested in his lifeguard shorts, and he and Dutchy loaded the jet ski onto the trailer attached to the buggy before Dutchy drove it back to the tower, leaving Mei and Jet alone at last.

'That's a very generous present,' Mei said as she watched An Na lie on her surfboard and start paddling. 'She will love it.'

'Should I have asked you about it first?'

She wanted to say yes but she knew it didn't really matter. 'No. It's fine.'

'Are you sure? I saw your expression when An Na unwrapped it; you didn't look as enthusiastic as I'd hoped.'

'It's not about me. An Na loves it; that's what counts. To be honest, I was just a bit miffed that you chose such a great present. You don't think you're spoiling her?'

'I probably am, but it's Christmas! I figured there's no better time and, just so you know, I plan on spoiling you too,' he said as he reached for her hand. 'You have given me the most amazing gift—our daughter. My life has taken a new direction with you and An Na. I want to see where it takes me next and I'm hoping that we can take that step together.

'Your family has welcomed me…you've supported me and shown me what a family can be. I'm never going to have the close relationship with my parents that you have with yours, but I've accepted that and realised that's okay. I have my sisters but now you have given me a chance to have a family of my own. If you'd asked me before I knew about An Na, I would have said I wasn't ready for that, in fact, I'm pretty sure I did say that, but now I can't imagine life without her. But I also can't imagine my life without you.

'You make me want to be a better person. You make me believe I can be that person. You inspire me to try harder, achieve more. With you beside me I feel that I can accomplish so much. I promised to take care of An Na—I want to make the same promise to you. I want to know if you think we could be a real family. Not just parents to An Na but if we could raise her together, as partners. As a couple.'

'A couple?'

Jet nodded. 'You and An Na have completely changed my life. I adore An Na—she is incredible, she is funny and warm and smart and I love her, and I feel the same way about you. I love An Na and I love you, Mei.'

'You love me?'

'I think I've loved you since the day I met you, but it's taken me until now to figure that out. When we first met, I was lost and lonely. The family I knew was gone—Lily was in

Sydney, Poppy was in Brisbane and Daisy was only fourteen. Ryder, who was like my brother, had moved to Perth, three thousand kilometres away, and I was living by myself in a caravan. I needed something—someone—but I wasn't expecting you. I didn't realise at the time what a gift you were. I was young and foolish and stupidly thought there would be plenty of girls like you out in the world, but after all this time and all my travels I've never found anyone like you.'

'There must be dozens of women like me—dozens of women better than me.'

'No, you are the only one for me. You are more than I deserve. You are strong, you are brave, you are smart, you are loving. I found my tribe with the lifeguards, but I still needed to find my soulmate. I needed to find the love of my life, the person who gives me purpose and that is you. I want to be the husband and father you and An Na deserve,' he said as he dropped to one knee.

'What are you doing?' Mei had forgotten about An Na, she was unaware of anything and everything else around her. All she could see was Jet, blond, tanned and gorgeous, kneeling in the sand at her feet.

He took her hand. 'I'm asking you if we can raise An Na together. I'm asking you to marry me.'

'You want to marry me?'

'I do. I want us to be a real family. I am already An Na's father but I want to be your husband. I knew you were special when I first met you. I believe we were destined for each other, there was a reason you fell pregnant, we are meant to be together. I love you and I want to build a life with you if you'll have me.'

'I used to hope that I'd find someone to share my life with, someone who would love me and An Na, someone who would want to be part of our future, but I never dreamt I would find you again.'

'And now that you have, now that we've found each other, what do you think?'

'I think you can make me stronger, braver and happier and I know I love you too.'

'Is that a yes? Will you marry me, Mei? Will you be my wife?'

'Yes. I will marry you.' Mei's eyes filled

with tears and they spilled from her lashes as she nodded.

Jet stood up and wrapped his arms around her. He kissed her soundly and Mei was vaguely aware of the sound of cheering and clapping. Jet spun her around and standing behind her she saw her entire family and Jet's sisters and most of the lifeguards.

'Where did they all come from?'

'I was hoping you'd say yes, and I thought you might like to celebrate with everyone.'

'They all knew?'

Jet nodded. 'I had to speak to your parents. I needed to know if I was who they had in mind for a son-in-law, and then I had to talk to Su-Lin—I thought she could give me an idea about whether you'd accept—and then I needed to have Ryder on stand-by, because I figured An Na would want to go surfing. And of course he had to tell Dutchy and Gibbo and Poppy my plan and then she told Lily and Daisy. You don't mind, do you?'

'What, that I was the last one to know?' She smiled.

'Almost the last,' he said as An Na and Ryder came out of the water.

'Mummy, why are you crying?' An Na asked.

Mei bent down and hugged An Na. 'Because I'm happy. Daddy and I are getting married!'

'You are?' An Na threw her arms around Mei as she lifted her up.

Jet kissed An Na's forehead. 'An Na was the last one to know,' he whispered to Mei. 'I wasn't sure how good she was at keeping secrets.'

Mei laughed. 'I think you made a good decision—on all counts.'

'Did Father Christmas tell you to marry Mummy?' An Na asked.

'We might have had a little chat about it,' Jet told her with a grin.

'This is going to be the best Christmas ever!'

'I'm glad you think so.'

'So now can we live with you?'

'Yes.'

'All right!' Gibbo's booming voice carried over the gathering. 'I know you've all got Christmas Eve dinner to get to but the champagne is on ice if you want to come up to the tower for a quick toast.'

'We've *all* got Christmas dinner?' Mei and An Na were having dinner with Jet and his sisters to celebrate Christmas, as all the Carlsons had offered to work on Christmas Day, but Mei was confused about Gibbo's use of the word 'all'.

Jet took Mei's and An Na's hands as they headed for the tower. Ryder was bringing An Na's board in the buggy. 'Lily has invited your parents and Bo and Su-Lin and the kids to join us. We thought we could have a proper celebration.'

Mei smiled. 'You really are embracing family life.'

'Completely.'

Gibbo waited until everyone was crowded into the tower and the champagne had been poured before he raised his glass to make a toast. 'Firstly, I'd like to congratulate Jet on his choice; you are a lucky man. Mei, you've got yourself a good, genuine, honest and kind man and I have no doubt he will be the perfect partner for you. I'm sure the two of you and An Na and any future additions to your family will all be very happy. Congratulations to you both. To Mei and Jet.'

Everyone raised their glasses and repeated, 'To Mei and Jet,' as Jet kissed Mei again.

'And secondly,' Gibbo added, 'I'd like to congratulate Jet on his promotion. Three cheers for that! Hip hip hooray…hip hip hooray…hip hip hooray!'

'Promotion? What promotion?' Mei looked at him.

'I have a bit more news. You know Gibbo and Paula are moving to Melbourne?'

Mei nodded. Paula had taken a promotion in her job which meant a move interstate.

'Obviously that means Gibbo's position as Senior Lifeguard is going to need filling. I applied for the position and I've been offered the role. You're looking at the new boss.'

'Really? That's fabulous—congratulations!' Mei threw her arms around Jet. 'What does that mean, exactly?'

'More responsibility and a pay rise. But the best thing about it is I get to manage the rosters.'

Mei frowned. 'Why is that a bonus?'

'Because it means I can plan my shifts

around yours and also around my sisters' shifts so that, between us and your family, there will always be someone around for An Na. Which means, my future wife, that if you still want to, you can apply for a post-grad medical school position and know that the rest of us will work around your study and paramedics commitments to take care of An Na. You can follow your dream.'

Mei eyes filled with tears. Again. She was turning into a fountain.

'What's wrong?' Jet's voice was filled with concern.

Mei shook her head and smiled through her tears. 'Nothing. Everything is perfect. I can't believe you're doing this for me.'

'I would do anything for you, Mei. I'm getting to follow my dream and you should get that too. I want us to show An Na that anything is possible. Your parents dreamt of a better life, a more stable, secure life, for you and Bo when they moved to Australia. I know you regret not studying medicine and I want you to have that chance. I don't want you living with regrets. I want to support you

and I want us to live our best life. Together.
How does that sound?'

'That sounds wonderful. I can't wait. I
love you.'

EPILOGUE

'HOW LONG UNTIL we see Daddy?'

She knew An Na wasn't asking because she was bored but because she was excited to see Jet.

The race had started over three hours ago but Mei hadn't even attempted to watch the whole event. It was impossible for two reasons. One, a lot of the race was out on the water and the only way to see the action was on one of the big screens set up along the promenade at Bondi Beach and two, there was no way An Na's concentration would have lasted the distance. The final leg of the race was a ten and a half kilometre run which looped past the lifeguard tower three times. Mei knew that watching the last leg would be enough for An Na and it meant they could cheer Jet on from the sidelines.

Mei glanced over her shoulder towards the beach, but she couldn't see the water through the crowds. She looked up at the big screen and saw the first competitors jumping off their boards as they came out of the ocean. 'Not long now.'

Ryder had saved them a space at the finish line near the lifeguard tower and they were right at the front of the barrier, about twenty metres from the line. They would have a good view of Jet as he ran past.

'Help me with my sign, Mummy.' An Na was struggling with a huge cardboard sign that she'd spent hours decorating with drawings of fireworks, surfboards, medals and a sketch of Jet.

Mei unrolled the sign, before rolling it up in the opposite direction to flatten it out, and passed it back to An Na.

Mei watched the first runners on the big screen. They were about to come past for the first time. She could see Jet. He wasn't at the front, but he was part of the leading pack. 'Here he comes.'

An Na was jumping up and down beside her, holding her homemade sign above her head as Jet ran towards them. 'Daddy! Daddy! You can do it. Catch up!'

He was in fifth position. Mei willed him to go faster, do better. She really wanted this for him.

'Go, Daddy! Run faster!'

Jet raised a hand as he ran past them. Did he pick up the pace? Mei thought he closed the gap a little between him and the person in front.

Mei's eyes were glued to the big screen and her heart was in her mouth as the runners circled back around. The next time they ran past Jet was in third place. An Na was beside herself and Mei was also finding it hard to contain her excitement, although she felt sick at the same time. Could he do it?

He stayed with the leading pack as they approached for the third and final time. He needed to finish top two. He was now second.

Mei was cheering, her voice was getting hoarse but she kept yelling and didn't dare to uncross her fingers yet. There wasn't much distance between second and third but there also wasn't much of a gap between first and

second. He wasn't guaranteed a top two finish yet. Anything could still happen.

There were one hundred metres to go.

Mei and An Na were screaming now,
cheering Jet on.

He was sprinting as he ran past them, closing the gap on first place. Would he have
time to catch the leader?

It was a race to the finish line, the final
ten metres. Mei couldn't tell from her angle
who was in front.

She looked at the screen as the two of them
hit the finish line together and saw the rib-
bon streaming from Jet's waist.

He'd done it! He'd qualified for the World
Championships.

'Did he win?' An Na was asking.

'He won!' She grabbed An Na's hand and
pulled her through the crowd. 'Come on.'

Jet was at the finish line, searching for
them.

'Daddy! You won!' An Na threw herself at
him and wrapped her arms around his neck.

Mei reached out, ready to catch An Na,
worried that Jet's energy might be completely
spent and he wouldn't have the strength to

hold his daughter. But she needn't have worried. He shifted An Na to one side, holding her with one arm, and reached for Mei with his other hand. He pulled her towards him and kissed her.

She kissed him back. He was hot and sweaty and he tasted salty, but she didn't care. He had done it and she was so proud of him.

'Oh, my God, you did it! Congratulations!'

Jet was beaming. 'I did it for you. It's all for you.'

* * * * *